CHARLIE
FOXTROT

Code 11- KPD SWAT-Book 5

BY

LANI LYNN VALE

Dedication

This one is dedicated to my readers. If it wasn't for y'all, this book would have never been.

Acknowledgements

FuriousFotog: You never cease to amaze me with your greatness.

Jonny Reid: You take a wonderful picture, sir!

Asli- I couldn't thank you enough for all the hard work you do for me.

CONTENTS

Charlie Foxtrot

CHAPTER 1

I don't know why people think I'm such a dick. I'm a fuckin'
delight to be around.
-Secret thoughts of Foster

Foster

"I need to speak to the officer that gave my grandfather a ticket. Right now," I heard snapped over the phone.

I shook my head and stood up out of my chair.

"I'll be there in a minute, Pat," I said tightly, reining in my anger as best I could.

Pattie Hightower was the front office receptionist who sat behind the wall of glass. The first person the general public saw once they entered the building.

She had a shit job, and didn't make enough. Everyone in the precinct was guilty of abusing her niceness, myself included.

Limping around the desk, I winced as my leg started the familiar aching burn that usually came around when I'd done too much work with it.

Which I had.

I did every day, but today I'd re-qualified with the SWAT team.

I'd run the obstacle course that every new potential member of SWAT had to run to be accepted into the fold.

I'd previously been on the SWAT team, but an incident last Valentine's Day with the crazy bitch that tried to take my brother, Miller's, and my sister-in-law, Mercy's, life had sidelined me temporarily.

Linda Moose, a.k.a. Crazy Bitch, CB for short, had tried to plow her car straight through Mercy's face.

At the time, Mercy had been pregnant with my nephew. I'd seen her small body fold into my brother's, and before I knew it, I'd started running.

Right into the path of the stupid bitch's bumper.

CB had reversed, so I had, too.

I'd stopped when my back had met the brick mailbox. Unfortunately, Linda had not.

She backed straight into me, pinning my left leg in between the bumper and the brick mailbox from hell.

Then she'd tried to leave.

Bad for her, my gun had been in my hand before I'd even consciously thought about it.

I'd shot her through the back glass.

The first two bullets had passed through her left shoulder, and the next one had grazed the top of her head.

She'd crashed after my last shots took out her tires.

It was inconclusive whether she passed out from hitting the tree, or the bullet to the head.

Regardless, I'd managed to stop her before my leg finally realized there wasn't much left to stand on.

I'd fallen to the ground and promptly passed out.

Then had woken up in a hospital bed ten hours later, legless, and in a perpetual bad mood.

"You got a live one, Crush," Chief Rhodes said, eyes alight with laughter.

I didn't bother to respond.

I'd somehow become the laughing stock of the station.

They thought it was funny to call me Crush.

I, on the other hand, thought it fucking sucked.

I didn't need to be reminded on a daily basis that I was missing my leg. Well, half a leg.

I had a below the knee amputation.

Which was better than, say, an above the knee amputation. Regardless, it was still an amputation and it had impacted my life greatly.

I witnessed the fact every morning when I looked down. Every morning when I fitted the prosthesis on my leg. Every morning when I walked into work.

My prosthesis looked like anybody's leg when I was wearing jeans or long pants. The problem was, was that everyone on the force, as well as in the community, knew I was missing a leg. Knew the weakness I had.

"No, I just want to talk to him. It won't take but a minute," I heard a woman's voice say once I reached the lobby.

Pushing the door closed behind me, I walked up behind the woman, surveying her.

She was around five eight or nine. Full figure, round hips, perfect ass. Long legs encased in tight jeans.

Curly, white blonde hair that was nearly the shade of mine came down to her mid back.

The ends looked like they'd been dipped in purple paint.

"Can I help you?" I asked the woman.

She whirled around, her eyes narrowing on my face, then taking in my badge, gun, and posture before returning her eyes to my mine.

My breath caught as I got a load of her face.

She was fucking *beautiful*.

Her eyes were the shade of warm, melted honey.

Her lips were luscious, and she had the cutest cleft in her chin that I'd ever seen.

And that was saying something, since my nephew and niece had cleft chins. That was hard to compete with.

I wanted to touch it. *Badly*.

But then her snotty attitude cleared that want right up.

"You're Officer Spurlock? Badge number 654?" She asked, crossing her arms across her breasts.

I raised my brows at her.

She obviously had done her homework about me.

Looking down at my badge, I pointed towards it with a finger. "That's me."

She moved forward, closing the distance I'd left between us in milliseconds.

"Let me tell you something, Officer Spurlock. What you did was despicable," she hissed.

I raised my eyebrow at her. "And what did I 'do,' exactly?"

"You gave my grandfather, a veteran, and a fine man, a ticket for having a pocketknife on him," she spat.

I blinked.

What the fuck?

"Are you talking about that crazy old man that was wielding a butcher knife at me? That was anything *but* a 'pocketknife.' It's closer to a machete than a pocket knife," I clarified.

Her eyes narrowed. "That was a pocket knife."

I gritted my teeth and pulled my phone out of my pocket. I'd show her how much of a 'pocketknife' it wasn't.

I flipped through my pictures, past the ones of my brother who thought it'd be funny to post a picture of his ass on my phone, over the stack of beer cans we'd used to make a tower, and finally stopping on the one I was searching for.

"Does this," I said, holding my phone out to show her the picture. "Look like a pocketknife to you, ma'am?"

Her brows lowered in confusion. "N-no. That's not what he just told me…excuse me."

With that, she pushed past me.

Caught off balance, I instinctually put my weight on my bad leg, and promptly ate dirt.

The woman was gone before I even hit the floor.

I was able to catch myself before I did any major damage to my person, but not in enough time to prevent the entire station from seeing me fall.

There were men lined up behind the counter, all of their eyes wide as they looked at me, wondering what they should do.

I could practically hear their thoughts.

Should we help him?

Can he get back up by himself?

Oh, my God. That woman just made the cripple fall.

Narrowing my eyes on them, I stood, making sure no one saw how awkward it was to actually stand, and walked out of the door.

Once I reached the front steps, I crossed my arms and watched as the woman yelled at her grandfather. The old man that looked like the most innocent man in the world.

The man who'd pulled the knife on me quicker than I could blink.

He was lucky all I gave him was a weapons citation.

I could've arrested him for threatening a police officer with intent to harm.

When she spotted me, she started to march up the steps, coming to a stop two down from me.

"He tells me you're lying. That he had nothing more than his pocket knife," she held up a fucking switch blade.

I reached for it, and she warily placed it in my hand.

Acting quickly, I pressed the lever, disengaging the blade and scaring the shit out of her.

"This," I said, holding my hand out to her, offering her the hilt of the blade. "Is a switchblade. This is not a pocket knife. It's also illegal, because it's double sided."

She looked at the knife now in her hand, then offered it back to me.

"Just keep it."

I took the blade from her hands, collapsing the blade, and shoving it in my pocket.

"What the fuck, grandpa! That's illegal, too!" I heard just before she dropped down into her nineties model Camaro and closed the door.

I couldn't help the smile that overtook my face.

For the first time in months, I had something to smile about.

CHAPTER 2

I hope a bird shits on your car.
-Blake to Foster

Blake

"Way to go, Blake!" I cheered myself on. "Make yourself look bad when you're about to start working there. There's a good idea!"

Jesus Christ.

Fucking grandpa.

I should've known he'd lie about that.

He was a shit like that sometimes.

Bursting through my mother's door with Gramps at my heel, I immediately shouted, "Mom!"

My mother was in her fifties and the proverbial 'housewife.'

She stayed at home while my father brought home the bread money, stating that she was staying at home to take care of the kids.

Even now he was still working, and she was still keeping house.

I found my mother in the kitchen rolling pie dough out on the counter.

My mouth watered, and I got distracted from what I was going to tell her.

"What kind of pie are you making, mama?" I asked, leaning over her shoulder to look.

Peaches were sliced on the counter, and I think I zoned out for a few seconds, because I only caught the second half of her sentence.

"…the garage. Would you mind?"

"I'm sorry, what?" I asked, shaking my head and backing away from the food.

I was on a diet, and I was determined to stick to it this time, no matter what.

"I asked if you'd go get me the potatoes from the garage. Are you staying for dinner tonight?" she asked.

I went to the garage and grabbed the potatoes, giving my gramps a glare when his eyes looked up from his car he was tinkering with.

"Um, no. I'm not," I told her.

If I stayed, I was fairly positive I wouldn't be able to skip the pie. I had willpower…kind of. Just not that much.

"Oh, that's sad. Are you going out with David for dinner?" She asked. "He called here looking for you."

I gritted my teeth, smoke nearly pouring out of my ears.

"Actually, mom, no. I'm not planning on ever having dinner with David again, if I can help it. My next lifetime would be too soon." I told her, turning my back on her pity filled face.

David was my ex-husband.

He was a cop with Kilgore Police Department, and we'd been divorced now for nearly a year and a half.

"I don't know why you have to be so uncivil towards each other," my mother admonished.

The tick that only ever came on when I thought about David started back up.

David and I had fallen in love when we were teenagers.

We got married when he was twenty one and fresh out of the police academy, and I was twenty.

I'd gone the housewife route, although we'd never had any children. *Thank God!*

I'd thought that we had an awesome relationship, too.

I'd been so proud to be known as a police wife. The woman who stood behind her man. Supported him in his every endeavor

Then he started working 'mandatory overtime.'

It started out as just here and there, and slowly morphed into over eighteen to twenty hours of extra time per week. At first, I hadn't been suspicious.

Then little things started to stand out.

How he started changing at work and coming home freshly showered and shaved.

How he'd be super sneaky with his phone, putting a passcode on it and forgetting to tell me the code.

Then there were the random purchases on our account.

Thirty dollars here at a flower shop. A hundred and fifty dollars there at a jewelry shop.

When we'd first started our life together, David had been the one in charge of the finances.

I'd trusted him to do what he needed to do, and had never needed to check our bank account.

We lived modestly in a house his parents provided us when we got married. I also stayed home most of the day, rarely venturing out to do anything other than get groceries or essentials.

Most of the things we needed I waited for David to do with me.

But then he'd started being gone a whole lot more and I started to get suspicious.

I don't know if he thought that just because I was a blonde, and that I only had a high school education, that I was stupid. But I most assuredly wasn't.

I'd been taking online classes here and there throughout our relationship. Also, before I'd even graduated high school, I'd had nearly enough hours to graduate with an associate's degree.

I'd been in the top ten percent of our class when we'd graduated, so I wasn't really sure if he was just that oblivious to my abilities, or if he thought his superior cop skills kept me from seeing what was going on right in front of me.

Needless to say, I finally caught on, two years after denying it, and confronted him.

One of the days he was supposed to be at work, I followed him. Right into the arms of his 'beat wife.'

A beat wife is someone you have while you're on patrol.

Berri Aleo was *that* woman.

David had met her while he was on his patrol, and he visited her nearly every day while he was on duty, and on his 'overtime,' for two years before I finally called him on it.

He'd been so surprised when I'd moved out of the house, emptied the bank account, and filed for divorce, all in one day, that he'd been in tears.

Apparently, he didn't love the other woman and it was all a huge mistake.

Whatever the fuck it was, I wasn't going to be a part of it. I'd lost all respect for him.

We'd been separated for a year and a half, and 'officially' divorced for six months.

Luckily, my uncle was able to get me a job at the PD as a dispatcher. Something I was supposed to start tomorrow morning.

I expected to be getting a call from him any moment, though, telling me I'd lost the job before I ever even truly had it.

It's not like I wanted to deal with listening to David on the police scanner all day long, but I'd do it if it got me money. Something I was in desperate need of, thanks to him.

"Well, on that note, I've got to go. You need to talk to grandpa about his knife problem, though. He lied to me, the old coot. I still can't believe he did that," I snapped, eyes on my grandfather working merrily through the window to the garage.

"Your grandfather was a cop for fifty years. He can lie to the best of them still. And he's always carried that knife around with him. There's no talking him out of it. It's supposedly something really special," my mother said, placing her pie dough into a pie plate and pressing it into the sides.

"Hmmm," I wondered. "If it was special, I didn't know. I gave it to the cop that gave him that ticket. He said it was illegal."

"It is," my father said, coming into the kitchen. "He should know that."

He followed up that comment by hanging his gun belt up by the back door, and hanging his hat beside it.

My father was a state trooper for the State of Texas. At fifty nine, he still looked pretty badass and intimidating in his uniform.

"On that note, I'll see y'all later before Uncle Darren gets here...oh shit." Uncle Darren pulled up in his police issued vehicle, and I darted for the backdoor.

Running around the house, I came up to the side and waited until Uncle

Darren climbed the front steps before I hightailed it to my car.

Luckily, Uncle Darren didn't block me in. Something he should've done if he'd wanted to talk to me.

However, there was no reason for him to be here unless he was wanting to talk to me.

Something I most definitely didn't want to do with him right at this moment.

"Bye, honey!" My grandpa called from the garage.

I waved at him and blew him a kiss before I dropped into my car, slamming the door behind me.

I backed out of the driveway and cringed when I saw my uncle on the porch watching me leave. His hands were at his hips, and I prayed he wouldn't follow me.

I already felt stupid enough.

I'd intended to go in to this afternoon with a lot more tact.

Then that man with his incredible smile and beautiful brown eyes had looked at me like I was the stupid blonde that everyone thought I was, and I lost it.

I just hoped I didn't have to see him anytime soon.

I'd be lying, though, if I really believed that.

CHAPTER 3

I like big...batons...and I cannot lie.
-Blake's secret thoughts.

Foster

"Unit 4. Possible 223 at 555 Wimberly Lane," the dispatcher said through my mic.

Even the shitty radio couldn't stop my cock from hardening as I heard *that* voice through my speakers.

Fuck.

I hadn't known she was a dispatcher.

Motherfucker. Was she new?

"10-4. Unit 4 responding," I said, pulling into traffic and heading to the opposite side of town.

Normally, this would've been Luke's, my boss and head of the SWAT team, beat. Today, though, he was tied up in an officer involved stabbing.

Although we'd all responded, Luke had been the first on scene, and had been the one to witness the act.

Chief Rhodes had sent him home for a day of R&R, which meant the rest of the cops on duty had to pick up the slack. Not that it was hard or bothersome. It wasn't. It'd just take me longer to get there than usual.

"Motherfuc-," I heard through the mic before the sound was abruptly cut off.

I smiled, knowing that the dispatcher knew exactly who it was that she'd just dispatched.

I arrived on scene with little fanfare, pulling up to the house in question, and stepping out of my car.

Yet again, my leg took a few seconds to work properly, but I was doing pretty good, considering.

I heard the fighting between the couple that lived there immediately after stepping out of my car.

My eyes scanned the area, taking in the two men under their front porch's awning two doors down from the house I was responding to. As well as the older couple at the windows of their own house directly behind me.

I suspected they were the ones that had called the cops.

Old people were busybodies like that.

Most of the crime watchers, I'd found, were old. They were the ones that were home the most. Sure, there were a few young ones interspersed throughout, but by far the most prevalent was the elderly.

Mostly because they wanted to live their lives in peace.

Something they were most definitely not getting right now due to the 'whore fucker' this and the 'cock sucker' that coming from the home in front of me.

Walking up the walk, I stood just to the side of the door, and knocked.

"Who is it?" The man bellowed.

"KPD Police. Can you come out here, please?"

I'd tried for stern and menacing, but I wasn't sure how much actually got through the fighting, as well as the door.

This time, when I knocked, I made sure to put a pound behind it, rattling the doorframe with its intensity.

The fighting stopped instantly, and two large, pounding feet made their way to the door.

Stepping back, I crossed my arms over my chest and waited.

Which I didn't have to do long by the way the boots hightailed it to the door.

A man in his thirties, dressed in shabby clothes that looked like they needed to be washed a month ago, yanked open the door.

Eyes wild, he asked, "What?"

"I've had a complaint of the fighting that was going on over here. Where is the woman you were fighting with?" I asked, staring around him into the house.

It was trashed. Tables overturned. Lamps on the floor. Glass figurines smashed to smithereens.

The woman was behind the man, peaking around a wall.

At the mention of her, her eyes got wide and she started forward.

"Renee, get over here so he can see I'm not hitting you," the man said.

'Renee' walked out slowly, coming towards the man and the door like it was the very last thing she wanted to do.

"Can you tell me what's going on here?" I asked, taking in the two.

"Yeah, my girlfriend," he spat. "Kicked me out of the house because I supposedly cheated on her. I've been living in a tent in the backyard. Then I find out that she's been seeing some bitch for two fucking months, having sex in our bed while I been outside sleeping on the hard ground. Ain't gonna happen no more. This here's my house, and she's just going to have to move out. In fact, I was just about to call you. She needs to get gone."

"You're not married?" I asked for clarification.

The man and the woman both shook their heads.

"Whose name is on the deed? How long have you both been together?" I asked.

"Six months. And that would be me whose name is on the deed," the man said. "Need proof?"

I nodded.

"Yes, if you're serious about having her leave your property," I said carefully.

Twenty minutes later I had the girl in the back of my patrol car.

"Where do you need to go?" I asked.

I'd have let her find her own way, but she'd looked so damn pitiful walking down the street with a garbage bag full of clothes that I'd stopped and picked her up.

"I don't have anywhere to go," she cried.

I didn't feel sorry for her. She'd made her bed; she needed to lie in it.

She'd admitted to sleeping with the other man in her boyfriend's bed. There was no wonder that he'd kicked her out.

Hell, I'd have been a lot more livid about the entire situation than he had been.

Pulling a U-turn at the next light, I drove her directly to the mission.

She could stay there for a few nights before she was asked to leave.

"Alright, ma'am. Here you are," I said, getting out and opening the backdoor for her.

She got out warily, looking at the building as if it was a venomous snake. "I'm not going in there."

She sounded like a stuck up bitch…not that I'd tell her that.

"All units be advised, we have a BOLO out for a white male, late forties, black hoodie and blue jeans. Red and white Nike's. It's suspected that he robbed the convenience store on 3rd Street," my new favorite dispatcher said.

Without waiting for a goodbye, I got into my cruiser and got back on the streets, all under the hate filled eyes of the woman I'd just dropped off at the mission.

***

Blake

"Oh, my God. The first freakin' call and I say a curse word on the open air," I muttered into my sandwich.

"It's okay, honey. It won't be your last, either," Pauline, the woman that was training me, said.

Pauline was nearly ten years older than my twenty four, and had been working with KPD Dispatch for going on fifteen years now.

She was the 'best of the best' according to all the girls in dispatch, and I was kind of excited to be working with her.

I'd had a ton of fun in the four hours I'd been here, and I couldn't wait to go back.

Especially since I got to hear that sexy, growl of a voice that I'd learned was nicknamed 'The Crush.'

"Hey," I said, picking at my sandwich. "Can you tell me more about that guy? Foster?"

"Crush?" Pauline clarified, raising her brows at me in question.

When I nodded, she continued. "Not really much to tell. He's on the SWAT team. I'm sure you know everybody on the SWAT team is badass. Crush, though, is more than most. There's something about him since his accident that makes him so…unapproachable."

"His accident?" I asked worriedly. "What accident?"

She squinted at me. "Everybody knows about that. He was the cop that had his leg amputated a year or so ago."

My mouth dropped open.

"That was him?" I gasped.

Wow. He really didn't look like he was missing a leg.

In fact, I distinctly remember studying his boots yesterday, and there'd been two of them.

"He's missing a leg?" I whispered quietly.

She nodded, and I sat there stunned.

I'd heard about that.

Hell, everyone in Kilgore had.

It'd happened in front of about a hundred cops. Some of them out of state. Some of them on Kilgore's Police Department, some County Sheriffs. Some of them, like my father, were Department of Public Safety.

Hell, he'd even been the one to take the lady out and live to tell about it.

"Wow," I said quietly. "That's pretty amazing. I didn't know he was any different than what he used to be, though."

Pauline nodded. "He's a lot different. He doesn't play anymore. He's the force's top ticket writer. He picks up overtime that nobody else wants. Literally, he's *that* cop. The one that nobody wants to mess with. The one that everybody knows and cringes when they pass."

"Aww, be easy on the kid. He's had a rough year," my uncle said from behind us.

I inhaled half of my sandwich, very nearly choking to death, but my uncle was there. Always able and willing to save the day.

He slammed his palm roughly down on my back, knocking the bread loose from my windpipe, as well as a few teeth for good measure.

"Okay," I groaned, pulling away from him.

Was it just me, or was he hitting harder than he needed to?

"Oh, Chief Rhodes!" Pauline said, standing.

In the process, she knocked half of her lunch on the floor, and I barely contained the urge to roll my eyes.

They treated my uncle as if he were a celebrity, being the chief of police. However, if they only knew that he was a horrible cheater at the game Go Fish, and the funniest drunk in the world, they'd never look at him straight in the eyes again.

"Uncle Darren, what are you doing at work today?" I asked suspiciously.

My uncle narrowed his eyes at me. "Oh, just seeing how your day was going so far. Just making sure everyone is treating you alright."

I wanted to smack him.

He damn well knew that I didn't want to be associated with him.

I didn't want people to look at me differently.

I wanted to be me, not Chief Rhodes' niece.

Now they'd all treat me differently.

In fact, Pauline was already staring at me like I was a bug she didn't want to be anywhere near.

Great.

"Thanks for stopping by. You can go now," I said through clenched teeth.

He grinned at me. Seriously and truly grinned at me.

Then he left, leaving only damage in the wake.

By the end of the day, everybody knew I was the Chief of Police's niece.

Cops. Receptionists. 911 dispatchers. Felons.

It was fucking *perfect*.

CHAPTER 4

I solemnly swear that I'm up to no good.
-Blake before she eats a package of Oreos.

Blake

"Excuse me," I said, keeping my head lowered to block the rain from getting under my hooded raincoat and saturating my hair.

I was on my way home, descending the steps of the station, when I heard it.

"Sorry, darlin," an extremely familiar voice said to me.

Shivers, and not the good kind, stole down my spine, filling up my lungs, and squeezing them to where I could hardly breathe.

"David," I said, nodding at him.

I might have been able to leave, but there was another man there with David, and that was the man that I'd made a fool of myself in front of just a short week ago.

Had it already been a week?

This, luckily, had been the first time I'd run into both men, and I was grateful.

I loved my job, but there was no way in hell I was going to keep working there if I had to see David often.

I didn't have enough bail money to accomplish that feat.

I still, every night, thought about him.

Thought about all that I'd *thought* we'd had.

All that time I'd wasted being loyal to a man that didn't extend the same courtesy to me.

Then there was Foster.

The tall drink of water in the middle of a hot Texas summer.

He was freakin' *beautiful*.

His hair was wet from the rain, making it look more sandy blonde rather than snow white blonde. All those beautiful blonde curls were plastered to his head as he took me in.

Were they friends?

If they were, I'd never know Foster better. Even if I did have an incredibly high-school-like crush on him.

I couldn't be friends with someone that was friends with my ex. I didn't want anything to do with David at all, even second hand.

"Bye Officer Spurlock, good job today," I said as I pushed past them and started down the steps.

Foster had interrupted a hotel robbery in progress, answering the silent alarm that the receptionist had tripped the moment the crack head had asked her for the money.

"Thanks," Foster said, sounding surprised that I'd even offered the compliment.

I tossed him a smile over my shoulder, rain wetting my face, and said, "That wasn't anything more than a compliment, Officer Spurlock. Don't let it go to your head."

The last thing I saw before the rain really started to pour down was David glaring at Foster, and Foster staring at me with a smirk on his lips. One that promised more things to come.

I drove home in the near monsoon weather, past my old home that now had a different woman's car in the driveway, and pulled into my driveway that was on the next street over.

I'd looked and looked for a house that was anywhere but where I finally found one. But I literally couldn't find anything anywhere else.

What I received in the divorce settlement was enough to buy an affordable house just two streets over from my old home. Which is what I had to do. It was either that, or move completely out of Kilgore, and I wasn't giving that royal dickhead the advantage of seeing me squirm.

The very next week, the asshole had moved his 'beat wife' into my home, and proceeded to play house.

At least they hadn't gotten married…yet.

It was a joy to get to see the other woman every day, though.

My phone rang before I could get out of my car, and I decided to wait and answer it before I got out.

"Hello?" I greeted my mother.

"Uncle Darren wants you to meet him at dinner tonight. Bodacious," my mother said excitedly.

"Why?" I asked, confused as to why my uncle wouldn't have called me himself.

"He sent your dad a message on his cell phone. He's talking to the Mayor of Kilgore right now, and can't break away."

"Is it just him, or what?" I asked, studying my windshield as it started to rain a little bit harder.

I hated when it rained.

Seriously hated it.

When I was sixteen, I'd had a wreck during a thunderstorm.

It was nearly four hours after my accident that I was found pinned in the car.

But that four hours would haunt me forever.

When I'd crashed, I'd gone nose first into a ditch that was filled with water that was flowing fast.

I'd spent the time watching as my car was dragged further and further down a gulley as lightning struck everything around me.

I couldn't get out of my car because of the pressure the water kept on the doors, and I couldn't get one single window opened.

I'd been scared to death that I'd die that night, and ever since I'd had a phobia of thunderstorms.

Now, as a precaution, I carried flares in my car, as well as a glass punch that would help me get out if it was ever needed again.

That wasn't enough to counteract the fear that I felt every time I drove in the rain.

"It's raining," I hesitated.

My mother's voice became less cheery. "I know. He said he'd send someone out to get you."

I nodded, knowing I wouldn't get out of it now.

He wouldn't have been sending someone for me if it weren't important to him.

"Fine," I said. "What time?"

"Seven thirty. Your ride will be there around seven fifteen," she said excitedly.

"Okay. Do you know who it is?" I asked.

"Nope. He didn't tell your daddy that," she said evasively.

I should've known when the familiar red truck that I'd helped shop for pulled into my drive an hour and a half later that it wasn't going to be good, but I decided to be the bigger person.

Closing the door to my house behind me, and locking it, I made my way down the driveway carefully.

David got out and opened the passenger door, soaking himself to be the gentleman that we both knew he wasn't.

There must've been someone there, otherwise he never would've bothered to get out.

He never used to.

I ignored his outstretched hand and opened the backdoor.

I was surprised to find two men already back there, one of which I couldn't get out of my head no matter how hard I tried.

Without waiting for them to move, I climbed over Foster's lap, scooting my ass over his legs before I plopped down into the middle seat beside him.

Foster looked surprised, while the other man beside him, one that looked eerily similar to Foster, grinned.

"Hey, how's it going?" I asked the man, smiling at him.

He winked. "Pretty good. Although, I gave up the front seat so you could sit up there. Not so you could sit back here smashed between the both of us.

"So go back up there," I said, shrugging and turning my face forward.

The front door slammed with unnecessary force, and I couldn't help the smile that split over my face.

Fucking douche.

He deserved it, though.

I couldn't believe my uncle made me ride in this piece of shit truck. The one that had been my dream truck. The truck that I'd put nearly all of my savings into to put a down payment on it. The very thing that David had fought so hard for in the divorce.

I wanted to accidentally pee on his leather fucking seats.

I still couldn't believe that he'd won it.

He had a freakin' 2010 Camaro. Why would he get both the car and the truck?

I, of course, was allowed to keep the 1995 Camaro that I'd had since high school because I'd brought that 'into the relationship.'

The bonus was that David allowed his new woman to drive the new Camaro while I was stuck with a piece of crap that barely chose to run on some mornings.

But the absolute icing on the cake, the best, *most awesome thing*, was the freakin' lei he had hanging from the rear view mirror.

The very thing he refused to allow me to ever fucking do.

Things hanging from the rearview mirror are a distraction. I heard whined in David's voice.

Fucking asshole.

The rage still burned bright after all this time, and it was a good thing I couldn't act on all my inner thoughts.

"So," I said to the man beside me. The older one, not the one that set my girly bits to tingling. "What are we doing here tonight? I feel out of the loop."

He raised his brows at me, and in the light of the lamps overhanging the road, I could see the smirk on his face.

"Everyone that was in on the call this afternoon is getting treated to a dinner by the hotel owner," the man said. "My name's Miller Spurlock.

It's nice to meet you."

He offered me his hand, and I took it, shaking it like I was taught.

I wasn't a limp noodle kind of girl. When I shook hands, whether it be man or woman, I made it count. I grasped their hands like I fucking meant it. Not that Miller could tell I was squeezing hard.

I scanned my brain for a few seconds, and finally came up with the number. "Unit number three."

He nodded. "That's me. This is my brother."

I could tell by the laugh in his voice that he'd witnessed my outburst against his brother.

Great.

They were laughing at me now.

"We're going to the Bodacious off 42," David supplied helpfully.

I didn't bother to answer him.

I'd actually been giving him the silent treatment for a year and a half now. Only modifying it when my proper upbringing demanded me to address him.

It really seemed to work well with him, too.

If I'd known that it worked so well during our marriage, I'd have used it a lot more.

"Who is this guy? And why'd it have to be tonight?" I asked Miller.

I could feel a dark energy at my back, and it was sending excited tingles up and down my arms and spine.

I could practically feel his eyes roaming over my body, studying me, and taking in my every word.

"He owns about seventy hotel chains throughout the South. That one was his first that he opened," a deadly quiet voice said to the back of my head.

I squeezed my eyes shut, thankful that the darkness kept me from giving my feelings away to the men in the truck.

I turned in my seat until my back was flat against the backseat, allowing me to turn my head and see the man that I'd been avoiding looking at.

I knew the dark wouldn't phase him. Knew he'd be able to see me the second I turned my face to his.

Steeling up my walls, and shoving my feelings, as well as my fear of the storm down deep, I said, "Cool beans."

Cool. Beans.

Out of the massive amount of words I could've said, I chose to say the most juvenile thing I could possibly think of.

Four points for Blake!

Not.

The funny thing was, was that I could tell that he was amused by my words.

Something that sounded close to an 'asshole' was muttered from the front seat, and Foster's eyes turned from mine to the real asshole in the front seat, and I could see something exchanged between the two before Foster's eyes turned out the window.

I sat in silence for the next twenty minutes as David navigated through the winding roads that would lead us towards our destination.

If there was one thing I could say about David, it was that he had an awesome grasp on driving. He'd never once scared me while he was driving.

The harsh lights of the restaurant we were going to startled me short moments later as I thought about how David used to cater to my needs.

Never driving in the rain when we didn't need to. Never driving over the speed limit because he knew I was scared.

Then he had to go and open his mouth.

"Let's get this done before I need to get home to Berri. She's got some bad morning sickness," David said as he bailed out of the truck.

I froze in the act of getting out, heart shriveling up into a tiny, never to be repaired, broken mess.

Oh, God that hurt.

He knew it'd hurt, too.

That'd been why he said it.

Foster's eyes, the ones that took in everything, saw the hurt that I couldn't quite cover up.

He offered me his hand, not saying a word, and I took it.

Grasping onto it like a lifeline.

"You were married," Foster said as he helped me out of the truck.

I nodded.

"For nearly five years," I said quietly. "He refused to have kids with me."

"That's why you left?" He asked quietly, lagging behind to allow space in between David and me.

I shook my head. "I found out he was cheating on me. For nearly two and a half years."

His jaw worked, as if what he'd heard had disappointed him.

"I didn't know," he rumbled.

I shrugged. "Not many people do. And I've never seen you around, so I don't know why you would."

He didn't say anything as we made our way inside.

The first person I saw was my Uncle Darren.

He looked at me warily, as if he thought I'd flip the off the handle.

I glared at him, not even bothering to give him a hug.

He'd effectively ruined my night, just by that one tiny act.

But then I realized that my hand was still in Foster's, and my palms started to sweat.

Did I let go?

Would it be weird if I kept holding his hand?

Wow, his hand is big.

His fingers were nice and long, too.

He wasn't wearing a wedding ring, and the watch he had on was awesome.

I wondered if the dash marks glowed in the dark.

"Does your watch glow in the dark?" I asked, my mind blurting it out before I was even aware that I'd said anything.

He let go of my hand, and my heart suddenly lurched.

I was bummed that he'd let me go, but then his hand went towards my back as he steered me towards the side of the table that would have his back against the wall. I went in first, which trapped me in.

However, I found that I kind of liked the feeling.

It was a different feeling.

When David and I used to go out, I'd always been on the outside.

Something about me 'always needing to pee' and him not wanting to get up and down every five minutes.

"So how has your first week been?" Foster asked, an odd tone in his voice that made me look at him.

His eyes were on David's, two tables over, who was staring...well *glaring*, right back at him.

It was as if David was pissed that Foster was sitting next to me, but I wasn't sure I could tell you why.

The man was the one to fuck me over, not the other way around.

"Who's the hotel owner?" I asked to capture Foster's attention.

He nodded in the direction of the man in the three piece suit and tie sitting catty corner to David. "Old guy, 0300."

0300.

Military time.

"Do all cops use military time?" I asked.

I never could quite grasp the whole 2400 hours thing. It didn't matter how many times I tried to figure it out, it just wasn't happening for me.

Foster shrugged, and his indifference annoyed me.

The earlier nice guy was nowhere to be seen, and in his place was the same man that had looked at me like I was a dumb blond just a short week ago.

Dammit.

I was destined to be forever known as *that* girl.

"I was in the Navy," he said once the waitress served us.

I'd ordered sweet tea, while Foster had ordered a bottle of beer. Foster's, to be exact.

"You're drinking the same beer as your name," I said smartly.

His brother, who'd sat across the table from me, piped in with, "We're named after the beers."

My mouth dropped open. "That's cool! I was named after my grandmother's dog."

The two men stayed silent for a few moments, processing that, and finally asked, "Why?"

I shook my head. "I haven't a single clue. Blake is a boy's name, yet I've been called that since birth. I don't know what my parents were thinking."

"They were thinking," my uncle said, sitting down beside Miller. "That they liked the name, and it meant something to them."

"He was my grandmother's dog. Apparently, he saved my mom when she was eight months pregnant, alerting her to a carbon monoxide leak in the house. The dog died about two weeks before I was born because he was hit by a car, so they chose to name me after the dog," I explained more fully.

"Well, that's a shitty story," Foster muttered, taking a hefty gulp of his beer before placing it down and picking up his menu, effectively dismissing us.

Miller glared at his brother, or tried to at least. The menu blocked him from everyone's view but my own.

His face was weathered and tired, and a small tic was playing at the corner of his mouth.

His face was what I would describe as rugged.

He had a dark brown beard that covered the lower half of his face.

It wasn't unkempt like some, though. It was very well maintained, and the edges precise.

He had a scar along his right temple that extended into his hairline, followed by a small mole behind his ear.

I could barely make out what used to be an ear piercing, as well.

He certainly no longer had it, but it was nice to see that he used to be able to let loose.

"So, what do you want?" My uncle asked, his bushy eyebrows raised in question at me.

I shrugged.

That was the eighty three million dollar question, wasn't it?

CHAPTER 5

What's she have that I don't? A magic vagina that compliments the size of your micro penis?
-Blake's secret thoughts

Blake

I didn't bother saying thank you for the ride.

In fact, I was pretty sure that David tried his freakin' hardest to make the drive as horrible as possible.

First, he'd dropped the other two off first, effectively leaving me in the car with him, trapped and unable to go anywhere, for another ten minutes more than I wanted to be.

Then he'd driven erratically, purposefully hitting huge puddles, and accelerating a little too fast.

On top of it all, it'd started raining impossibly harder than it had been the moment I no longer had Foster as a buffer, allowing me to focus solely on the two things I hated.

David and the rain.

"Don't bother with Spurlock. He's a womanizing prick," David said, snottily, once Foster walked inside his door.

I didn't bother to glance up at him in the rear view mirror. There was no point.

That was rich, coming from him, but I wouldn't give him the satisfaction of allowing him to think he knew me.

He didn't know me.

If anything, handing that challenge over would only spur me on, not make me run the other way.

Regardless, I ignored him.

It wouldn't due to break my year and a half accomplishment of ignoring him.

"I tried calling you this weekend," David said, clearing his throat. "I want to know if I can have the bassinet. The one my father gave you before he died."

I blinked, turned to him, and smiled.

The evilest smile I could muster.

Yeah *fucking* right.

He could have that over my cold, dead body.

His dad was also an officer, and I secretly thought he'd always loved me more than his own son.

I'd admired the beautiful woodwork on the bassinet about a month before David and I had married, and Cary saw me admiring it.

Cary had bought it for me.

Had driven back three hours where we'd been not even a half day before, and had bought it.

He'd then given it to me as a wedding present.

Me. Not David.

"You're not going to be civil about this, are you?" David asked, pulling onto my street.

I shook my head.

No, I wouldn't be.

I'd loved Cary, and that was the only thing I had left of him, except my memories.

That was the one and only thing, besides my clothes, that I'd taken with me that day I'd left David.

He, of course, hadn't noticed it until he needed it, but that wasn't my fault.

Instead of pulling into the driveway, allowing me to get as close to the house as he could get me, he stopped in the middle of the road.

I got out.

The moment my feet hit the pavement and I turned to reach for my bag and umbrella, while David sped off in a hail of water.

Luckily, I'd had my hand around the strap of my purse, or he would've taken off with it.

"You stupid mother fucker!" I yelled, the rain soaking me to the bone.

Lightening rent the sky above me, and my heart started to pound as I sprinted for my front door, and refuge.

I was thankful for the overhang that shielded me from the rain, but I was still soaked to the bone by the time I got to my front door open.

"You're home! You're home!" My Macaw, Boris, crowed the moment I opened the front door.

I grinned.

Boris always had my back.

A loud boom of thunder shook the house, and I cringed against the couch.

"Boom goes the dynamite," Boris continued.

Boris wasn't a fan of loud noises, thunder and explosions from the TV included.

I'd gotten Boris when I'd moved into my new place, and was happy that I'd chosen to get him.

He was better than a freakin' watch dog.

Walking over to Boris' cage, I picked up a Cheeto and offered it to him.

"Thank you, Hot Mama," Boris called out before crunching the Cheeto into a mess of crumbs at his feet.

Boris also liked to call me 'Hot Mama.'

He'd called me that since the moment he'd heard the song *Hot Mama* on the radio during our drive home.

Apparently, the trip had been a memorable one, and my title stuck.

Covering up his cage after sending him a kiss through the air, I walked into my room, stripped down to my bra and panties, then went to bed.

My sleep was fraught with David stealing my bassinet, and the hot, angry brown eyes of Foster saving it for me while wearing a kilt and holding a sword.

He was a hero even in my sleep.

***

I woke up and went for a run.

My mind was in a fog the entire way.

So much so, that I ended up running right past David's house.

I saw him in the front yard, heading to his shift.

He had his arms wrapped around Berri's shoulders, holding her to him as he kissed the life out of her.

Something he used to do to me.

I ran harder, closing my mind off to where it was only me and the road.

Pushing my legs so hard that I was all the way down a country road before I even realized I'd gone way further than I'd intended.

I turned around, but instead of running, I started to walk.

That's when I realized I was on the same road where David had dropped off the two men yesterday.

It looked a lot different in the light of day, and with no water pouring down out of the heavens, but no one could mistake those bluebonnets.

They were so beautiful that I stopped and stared out over the open meadow.

I hadn't realized that I'd gained an audience until I heard a woman's amused voice from behind me.

"I still do the same thing every morning," the woman's soft, melodic voice came from my side.

I turned to find the woman standing there in her bathrobe, her morning paper in her hand.

"Yeah, I didn't realize we had somewhere like this in our town," I said stupidly.

The woman was beautiful, even in her bathrobe. Something I'd never, ever in my life, be able to accomplish.

Her long brown hair tumbled down over her back and shoulders in waves.

She had wide brown eyes and a soft smile on her face.

"We just moved in. The old owners didn't like to advertise that this was here, so not many know about it. Even the ones that have lived here their whole lives," she said understandingly.

I nodded. "I've lived here since I was five. I was sure I'd missed something. This doesn't just happen overnight," I said, waving my hand to encompass the woman's house.

She bobbed her head in agreement. "I agree. You're welcome to come up and check it out from the top if you'd like."

I shook my head animatedly. "No, I have to be getting back. I have to work in," I looked at my watch, eyes bulging when I saw that I had less than an hour to get back, get changed, and then get to work. "Shit. I'm late. Thank you for offering! Have a good day!"

I started out at a quick pace, but eventually had to slow way down when I realized I wouldn't be making it back at all if I didn't moderate my pace.

That was, of course, when I saw him.

He was shirtless, wearing only a pair of black track pants.

He had on bright neon green running shoes, but if I was being honest, that wasn't what had my attention.

It was the man's upper body that had my jaw dropping.

I swallowed thickly and kept my head down, surreptitiously glancing up as I got closer and closer to him.

Oh, God. His abs were magnificent.

I swear there were at least ten of them. Possibly even thirty eight...but who was counting?

Was that even possible?

And his shoulders and arms were massive. Not behemoth, I work out at the gym three times a day massive, but an honest massive. The kind you get from working your ass off doing hard labor and just living life.

Something I hadn't realized when they'd been hidden under those t-shirts he wore.

If that were me, and I had that smoking hot body, I'd be wearing shirts that accentuated it, not brought attention away from them.

Then again, I'd been praying since I was fourteen for boobs that extended over the B cup that I currently was, and I'd yet to see that eventuality.

I kept my eyes down as I passed him, but I didn't need to bother. He'd never even acknowledged me.

Not even an eye twitch.

Which only served to make my already depressed mood even worse.

That was when I decided that maybe I should just stop caring.

Maybe I was meant to be alone.

Maybe, just maybe, there was no one out there for me.

With that thought on my mind, I finally made it back to my house, *on time*.

Although, when I opened my front door, what I found made me late once again.

I could tell someone had been there.

Who, I didn't know.

Nothing was overtly obvious. Only little things.

A picture frame there. A candle here.

My computer was on, when I distinctly remembered turning it off.

Then there was the missing photo album.

The one I found myself looking at last night, torturing myself over what I used to have.

So I called the one person I knew would be there for me when I needed it.

My daddy.

CHAPTER 6

*Sticks and stones may break my bones, but lights and sirens excite
me.*
-T-shirt

Blake

They say that, as a dispatcher, you take calls that you'll never know the
outcome to.

They also say that dispatchers have to have a warped sense of humor
because of what they deal with on a daily basis. Kind of like cops and
firefighters do.

They're the first ones that make official contact with the patient.

They get no letters of commendations, no awards for saving a child from
a burning building.

What we had, though, was a sisterhood.

Our entire outfit was compromised of 15 women ranging in age from my
twenty four to the eldest at seventy one.

They all told me their stories. Some good, and some really, *really* bad.

I guess I never really thought about anything that 'bad' happening to one
of my callers.

I was all prepared for a car accident, or a woman in labor.

I hadn't had very many *'true'* 9-1-1 calls yet.

I'd had mostly stupid calls.

My car won't start. My power's out. I think my wife's sleeping with another man.

Why people would call 911 because of those things, I didn't know, but they freakin' did. Constantly.

So as I answered my line, ten minutes past midnight, never in a million years would I have thought that I'd hear what I heard.

"911, what's your emergency?" I answered, tracing the call the moment I could.

"There's someone in my house," a quivering teenaged voice said through my line.

I immediately started to dispatch a unit to her address.

"Can you tell me what's going on, honey? Where are you?" I asked her.

My voice didn't have even show a hint of the fear that was coursing through my veins. I was a fucking rock.

"I'm here alone with my little sister and big brother. My parents are away for the weekend," she whispered. "I live in apartment 1B. Town Royal Apartments."

I blinked, typing the information into my computer and immediately letting the closest responding officer know what was up.

"What's your name, honey?" I asked.

"Amy Lynn," she said shakily. "What's yours?

I assumed that was out of politeness that she asked, so, out of politeness, I answered her.

Typing in the information I was receiving I said, "My name's Blake. Now, Amy Lynn, can you tell me what you hear?"

She didn't answer, and I waited, hoping that what I thought was happening wasn't actually happening.

"Amy Lynn?" I asked after another few long moments of silence.

"Nobody in here," a deep male voice said gruffly. "Thought you said there was another girl."

"There is," a young man's voice said. "She must be gone with the parents. Let's just get the stuff and leave."

"Hmm," the gruff voice hugged. "Fill your bag."

My fingers were typing away furiously, letting the responding officer know what was going on, such as the number of assailants, and what I would guess their ages being.

Since this was my first official call by myself, I'd been left alone with barely anyone in the room surrounding me.

We ran a two woman crew. Both Pauline and I worked swing shift. Eight p.m. to four a.m.

I'd been informed that, on holidays that were busy 'run days', we'd get one more person to work with us. Calls on our shift were the busiest. It was when the crazies came out to play.

Like now, for instance.

Two people breaking into a house while children were quivering under their beds. Utterly defenseless.

"Ohh," a cooing voice said chillingly. "What do have here?"

"Amy Lynn," I whispered. "Amy Lynn!"

Then, an ear piercing wail rent the air, making me wince as the sound pierced my eardrum.

"Get off me!" the girl shrieked. *"Get your filthy hands off me!"*

Then, as if in a movie, she started to describe them. Almost like the girl did in Taken, the movie. Except Amy Lynn's detailed description was a lot more…colorful.

"You're so fucking ugly, with your stupid black hair, and your ugly brown eyes. You're ugly as fuck, and that green shirt is the worst I've ever seen. And where'd you get those stupid Khaki's? They're supposed to fit, not sag around your knees, you dumbass," Amy Lynn screeched.

My heartbeat started to pound in time with my fingers as I started freaking out.

On the inside, that is. On the outside, I was cool, calm, and collected. Mostly.

I switched my mic over to the police band, immediately letting the officers know what was going on, knowing that the shaking of my fingers wouldn't allow me to type right then.

"We need any available units to apartment 1B. Town Royal Apartments," I said, voice quivering. "They've found the girl."

Then I listened as the girl started to get beaten.

Slap after slap had me leaning forward and closing my eyes.

Each distinct smash of the perp's fists hitting Amy's body made my stomach roil, and tears push over the lids of my eyes.

***

Foster

"Dispatch, this is unit 4. I'm on scene. The front door's wide open with no one in sight. I'm going to breach the property," I said as I got out of my cruiser.

My gun was in my hand, held pointed at the ground, but at the ready, as I walked slowly towards the door.

The moment I entered the apartment, I knew the men who'd broken in were gone.

The boy who was suspected to be there, was on the couch.

His throat was slit from ear to ear.

Blood seeped into the couch as his hands clutched desperately at his throat.

"Dispatch, I have a 217. I need the FD. Priority one," I said urgently, dropping down to my knees beside the boy and picking up a blanket that was on the floor by the couch.

Code 217 was an assault with intent to murder. If I'd ever seen *anything*, *this* was intent to murder. On a grand scale.

"Hold this on the wound," I said. "I'm going to clear the house."

Normally, I would've done that first, but the scared look in the boy's eyes had me breaking protocol all over the place.

I touched his head and walked slowly to the back bedrooms.

The hallway from the living room had two ways I could choose. Left led to a single door on the very end that was closed, and right led to a bathroom that I could see straight into, and a bedroom with the door standing wide open.

I could see a girl's legs, covered in bright pink princess socks on the floor, and bile rose in my throat.

Oh, Jesus.

I moved slowly, pieing the corner as came up to it.

The term 'pieing' was said when a person, such as myself, backed up until he could see around the corner, but the person on the other side could not. It was meant to offer protection as well as give you an idea what was on the other side without exposing your head or anything vital to the other side.

My eyes swept the room in a fast arc before I dropped down to one knee beside the little girl.

I was so relieved to find a heartbeat that I nearly dropped my gun.

The only thing that seemed wrong with her was the fact that she had a large goose egg on her forehead.

That's when I saw the other girl.

The teenager that must've been the one to call.

She was beaten to a pulp.

Her face, arms, and legs were a mass of bruising, standing out starkly against the white nightgown that was covering her body.

A nightgown that had been shucked up to her waist.

Luckily, though, it looked like the act had been interrupted, because the girl's panties were still in place.

After checking the teen for a pulse, I took a blanket from the bed, and gathered the little girl off the floor before placing her in the very corner of the room beside her sister. Then covered both of them with the blanket.

Then I went to the last bedroom.

Luckily, that room was clear.

I went back to the front room, checked the boy who was still amazingly awake.

"They're all right, boy," I said to him.

"Dispatch, the scene is secure. Send in the medics. Gonna need three," I said.

"10-4," a relieved Blake said over the airwaves.

A flash of green caught my eye, and I realized that what the man was wearing was a near exact match to what the teenager had described over the phone not even ten minutes before was dashing through the apartment complex.

"All units be advised," I said quickly. "A male subject fitting the description of the attacker just ran East through the woods behind the Royal Oaks Complex. Heading towards Main Street."

An hour later, pumped up on adrenaline and spoiling for a fight, I pulled into the Waffle House for my lunch break.

I took a seat at the bar, ordering myself a meal before I acknowledged the firefighters who'd had the same thought as I had.

"How's it going, Tai?" I asked the man beside me.

Tai was one of the responding medics to the scene. He was also the one to call me to let me know that all three children would be making a recovery. The two elder ones would have a rockier road than the youngest, but they'd all recover.

"I'm pissed. I can't fucking believe he got away," Tai said, shaking his head in denial.

I grimaced.

They'd caught one of the attackers. The one that'd been described, yet the other one was still at bay.

Still out there to do the same thing to another unsuspecting family.

The fucker we'd caught, Bruce Brenton, had refused to give up his partner.

Had also refused to talk without his lawyer, which meant we didn't get jack shit.

The good thing, though, was that he'd be getting a really nice prison sentence. Assaulting a child was a felony, and he'd be spending a lot of time up close and personal with his fellow inmates for the next thirty years, if I had anything say about it.

I knew a lot of people, and I'd make damn sure that the man never saw another peaceful day in his life.

"I agree," I said.

Tai's food was placed down in front of him, followed by mine a few minutes later.

The other firemen sat at three booths at our backs, but we didn't join in on their conversations. Both of our minds on what we'd heard and seen today.

Sometimes, the job of a police officer, firefighter, and hell, even a dispatcher, was a hard pill to swallow. A lot of times the good guy didn't win.

A lot of times, we were the ones to pick up the pieces, and that wasn't a very fun job.

But there were those times where the rewards outweighed the benefits. Times when the good times outweigh the bad.

Those times were what kept us going.

Kept us sane and happy. Doing the job that was every bit as rewarding as it was exhausting.

"Your dispatcher. She did well," Tai said after he finished his food.

"She's not my dispatcher," I muttered, not bothering to look up from my food.

"That's not what I heard you say to her after you got those kids to the hospital. 'They're gonna be alright, baby' over the airwaves shouts 'MINE!' to me," Tai said.

I shrugged. "Whatever."

I hadn't meant to say that.

It'd just happened, and I'd heard it from everybody that was on tonight.

Fuck me, but I didn't know why my mouth said the things it did.

I just felt like she'd want to hear it.

Next time, though, I'd make a point of actually calling her instead of saying it over the radio.

***

"Have you ever seen Final Destination?" Blake asked as I was driving her home later that night.

How I'd been the one to end up with her in my car, I didn't know. But it was the last thing I wanted to do. Especially with my mind in the state it was in.

What I really wanted to go do was go for a nice long run. A run where I tried to outpace my troubles.

I shook my head. "No, why?"

She pointed to the log truck in front of us.

The man was trying his hardest to stay on the road, but the wind from the impending storm was really throwing him all over the place.

"That," she pointed. "That right there. Every time I see a log truck, I think of that movie. The whole point of the movie is a couple of kids trying to cheat death. There was an order to it, and death went in that particular order. If it couldn't, fate found a way to make it happen. This particular scene is showing a couple driving with a log truck in front of them. It keeps zooming in on the chains holding the logs down, and suddenly they just snap."

I could tell where she was going with the story before she even made the snapping gesture with her hand.

"Anyway, the logs start falling off the truck, and it's like a chain reaction. Person after person dies. A brutal, horrible death," she whispered.

My eyes moved to her face quickly before returning to the log truck.

"I don't like thunderstorms," she said after a while.

Since I didn't know what to say to that, I stayed quiet.

Was that why she had a phobia of driving in the rain?

When we'd gone to pick her up the other day for dinner, I'd thought it weird that the chief had asked us to ride together. Now, though, I knew it was for Blake's benefit, it made a little more sense.

David had point blank asked the chief if Blake needed a ride, and the chief had purposefully told us to ride together so Blake didn't have to ride with David alone, and so she didn't have to drive herself in the rain.

The man was thoughtful, watching out for her left and right.

The curiosity, though, was killing me.

"Why don't you like storms?" I asked finally, not able to stand not knowing anymore.

She sighed.

"When I first got my license, I was driving home from a friend's house during a really bad storm and I wrecked my car. I ended up nose first in a ditch that was filled to the brim with flowing water, and stayed trapped in it for over six hours," she explained. "My car was the color of the water. A deep hunter green. I blended in, and I was in a part of the town that no one could hear my yells. Freaking lightening was touching down all around me, and I was so scared it'd hit the water and travel down towards me. It was the worst experience of my life."

"PTSD," I said softly. "That's what it sounds like."

She pursed her lips. "Maybe. But it doesn't hinder my daily living any. I just really, really don't like driving in rain. Or storms period. That doesn't mean I cower into a ball when one comes around. I will still drive in it, I just choose not to if I have the option."

I nodded. "Maybe that's it."

She frowned at me, but her scowl lacked the punch it would've normally had since the sky chose that moment to really let the sky open up.

Rain poured down.

Big, fat drops.

It was pouring down so hard that I had to slow the truck to allow the windshield wipers to keep up.

"This. I don't like this," she said, gesturing to the windshield and the weather beyond.

"Hmmm," I said, pulling down the same street that I'd been on just twenty four hours ago.

I pulled into her driveway, and pulled up as far as I could before I put it into park.

"Do you...do you want to come in?" She asked.

Her voice sounded so hopeful, and even though my mind was screaming yes, I knew what really needed to be said. "No. I'm sorry. I have somewhere to be."

***

Blake

I closed the front door, tears threatening to pour over my lids as I locked the door.

Why was I so undesirable to him? Why, at the mention of coming inside, had he flinched like I'd asked him to shoot himself in the foot?

What was wrong with me that no one wanted to be around me?

None of my friends from high school spoke to me anymore.

If David hadn't been so controlling, had been nicer, or more fun to be around, I wouldn't have had to choose him over my friends. I'd have someone to share my fears, hopes, and dreams with. Have a girlfriend or two to hang out with, to complain about how my ex ruined my life.

I, of course, had my parents.

But they weren't the same.

I just wished for…someone.

Someone that'd be there for me.

Someone that'd give me a hug when I needed it.

Like right fucking now. I needed a hug in the worst way.

Thunder rolled, and my heart pounded.

"Boom goes the dynamite!" Boris yelled.

Knowing I wouldn't be getting to sleep anytime soon, I went to my back room, and did the only thing that I knew would help me find relief.

CHAPTER 7

Never, ever, trust men. They're all the same. Big 'ol buttheads.
-Blake's note to self

Foster

"I cannot believe you're making me do this, Uncle Darren. This is Missy's job. Seriously, I'm going to give every single one of your SWAT team food poisoning, and then where would you be?" that voice said.

The voice that gave me an instant hard on.

The voice that'd been teasing me for weeks over the airwaves.

The voice that I wanted screaming my name with me pounding her to oblivion.

"Missy gave you very detailed instructions. All you have to do is right here," Chief Rhodes said to Blake.

I'm glad that I never did anything with her...or to her, that would've brought his wrath down on my back.

It was a good thing to know. Considering it'd been in all my intentions to seduce her...and possibly keep her.

"Alright, I've got the biggest pot I could find, boiling with water. Now what?" she asked, running her finger over a piece of paper at her side.

I glanced at Chief Rhodes and nearly laughed when I saw him flipping through what looked like a Guns & Ammo Magazine.

He wasn't even paying the least bit of attention to her.

Leaning against the door jam, I continued to watch as she brought out a large paper bag that had 'Fisherman's Cove' on the side.

Peeking into the bag, she squeaked and stepped back, letting the bag drop to the floor.

"Oh, my God! They're all over the floor, Uncle Darren!" Blake squealed.

The Chief didn't even look up from his magazine.

"Pick them up," he said distractedly.

The lobsters, all fifteen of them, started crawling around the kitchen floor.

"Uncle Darren, you big bastard," Blake hissed.

The Chief smiled. "Did you read this article yet?"

"Which one? The one on the fifty caliber AR-15?" Blake gasped, stepping to the side of a crawling crustacean.

"That one. Do you see how far the shot knocks him back?" the Chief laughed.

"About as far as I'm going to knock you if you don't fucking help me," she growled, dancing on the tips of her toes and shaking her head.

I scanned her body, taking in everything in a glance.

Her hair was up in messy bun on top of her head, stray hairs falling out every which way.

She was wearing blue jean shorts that just barely covered her ass, and a white tank top that said, 'I make dirt look sexy.'

Her legs were long and toned.

They were deeply tanned, but you could tell that they were tan from being outside, and not a tanning bed.

She had a suntan line at her ankles from what looked like socks and shoes.

Her toes were painted a lime green, and she was wearing a pinky toe ring.

The whole outfit was outrageous, but it fit Blake's personality perfectly.

"Need help?" I rumbled from the doorway.

The Chief didn't look up, but Blake did.

And she looked stunned.

"What are you doing here so early? Dinner's not ready yet," she snapped.

I held my hands up.

"I'm here because I'm supposed to drop these off," I said, waving a stack of folders in her direction.

My eyes roamed the front of her, zeroing in on the way her pink and white bra straps showed from under her tank.

She narrowed her eyes, and effectively dismissed me by turning her back on me.

I guessed, though, that it was because she was hiding the way her nipples pebbled in reaction to my gaze.

Well, I'll take that as she was happy to see me.

The Chief finally stood and walked over me, stepping over a lobster as he went. "You have one escaping into the kitchen," he said on his way out.

I followed him, smiling at the curse she tossed at his back.

"You're mean," I laughed.

The Chief looked over at me and winked. "She needs to be challenged sometimes. And she's stubborn as hell. If I hadn't given her something to do, she'd just be worrying."

He led us to the backdoor, and out onto the deck.

"Worry about what?" I asked.

He sighed and ran his fingers through his hair. "Her house was broken into last night. They took a couple of things. Little stuff. A vase she got for her wedding, and a picture album. Her computer was wiped."

I pursed my lips, thinking about what he said. "Is it related to the ex?"

He shrugged. "David was on shift last night, so we know it wasn't him. The girlfriend had an alibi. Not that I accused them of anything, but she made sure to offer one up."

I nodded.

My eyes scanned over his backyard.

It was nice.

Large.

Everything that I didn't want.

I wanted wide open space. I didn't want a place that was confined by a fence.

I wanted to be able to walk out my backyard, and not see a neighbor in sight.

What I also wanted was for my brother to stop worrying about me.

I'd been living with Miller and Mercy ever since my accident, and you'd think I was their child with the way they treated me.

Always making sure I was alright. Making sure I had every uplifting hand they could offer.

"Here," I said, handing over the files to him.

He took them, flipping it open and looking through it.

"Thanks," he sighed. "I was hoping to stay away from work for the next couple days, but I had a hunch and I was curious."

I raised my brow, wondering if he'd expand on it.

Which he did in the next second.

"David's girlfriend seemed really jittery when I ran into them at the diner, and there was something she said about the break in that made me wonder. So I had my secretary run her name in the database for me. Thanks for bringing them, by the way. I needed to help Blake with the lobsters," he said, laying the first file out on the table before he scanned it.

It sure looked like he was doing a lot of 'helping.'

Not that I would get into that. Not with the Chief of Police, anyway.

The man was my boss, after all. I wasn't stupid.

"And what'd she say that had you questioning her?" I asked, taking the bait he was handing me.

He shrugged. "She was so adamant that she 'didn't do it' that I started to not trust her word. So I had her and the friend, the one that was her alibi, checked out."

"And?" I asked.

He shook his head. "Nothing. Neither can be confirmed. It could be possible that they were with each other, but it could also be possible that they weren't, and that the friend is just covering for her."

I nodded. "What else is there?"

"Aleo's file has a few minor incidences. Three speeding tickets. A restraining order. That's it," he said, slamming the file closed and moving on to the friends.

"And the alibi?" I asked.

He flipped it open.

"Ronaldo Aleo. The ex," he said. "Couple of misdemeanors. Nothing else, though."

"Why would the two exes be hanging out together?" I asked, truly interested in knowing the answer.

I didn't know a single couple that'd divorced that was friendly with the other.

He shook his head. "They were discussing child support or something to that effect. He was over at her house, and that's all I got from them."

I nodded, but before I could ask any more questions, a shrill scream pierced the air that had both of us running into the kitchen.

CHAPTER 8

Friendship is like pissing your pants. Everyone can see it, but only you can feel its warmth. I want someone to be the piss in my pants.
-Blake's secret thoughts

Foster

We found Blake standing on the counter with a pair of grill tongs in her pot-holder-covered hands, and a lobster hanging from the very tips.

The lobster's front pincher was stuck in one of the grooves of the tong.

Blake had the lobster suspended over the large pot of boiling water, and she was crying.

"It won't come off!" Blake cried, shaking the tongs.

The scene was so unreal that there was only one thing I could do.

Laugh.

A laugh that I desperately needed.

I limped over there after I finally managed to catch my breath, and easily took the lobster off the hook and put him out of his misery.

That's when the screaming started.

"Oh, my God!" She cried, huge crocodile tears pouring out of her eyes. "Are you fucking kidding me? They scream?"

The Chief was in the corner, holding his stomach as he tried in vain to get his laughter under control.

"Where are the rest of them?" I asked.

She pointed to the floor.

"Where?" I asked again.

"Under the Tupperware," she said, gesturing to the plastic bowls all over the floor.

I'd originally thought that they were from her mad dash on the counter. Now I knew different.

Bending down, I flipped the bowl over to find one confused looking lobster.

Picking him up, and those of his brethren, I dropped them all into the boiling water, and covered the pot.

"Now what?" I asked.

Her eyes, though, were focused on the pot as the lobsters all thrashed around wildly as they were boiled alive.

"That would be such a horrible way to go. I don't think I can eat them. Not ever again," she whispered brokenly.

I shrugged and turned my face, which put me into the perfect place.

Staring at her *way* to short shorts. Shorts that I only had to tilt my head just right and I could tell she was wearing something purple. Shorts that were God's gift to man.

"I'm pretty sure they don't feel anything," I said, backing away, knowing if I didn't get out of there, and quick, I'd be sneaking my fingers up the miniscule pant leg and running my fingers through the lips of her sex. Sinking my thick fingers deep inside of her.

I stumbled, drawing Blake's attention from my face, down to my exposed legs.

Her eyes widened when she finally saw my lack of leg.

Saw the black graphite prosthesis that was so blatantly obvious that I couldn't help but cringe when people stared.

All thoughts of fucking her went out the goddamned window.

Who the fuck knew if I could even fuck normally anymore?

Who the fuck knew what was in store for me.

Everything, and I do mean everything, was different now that I was missing a piece of myself.

Walking. Driving a car. Getting out of bed. Taking a shower. Putting on motherfuckin' pants.

There was not one single thing that I could do easily anymore.

Everything took forethought.

I had to plan out my morning now, the night before.

Used to be I could just get out of bed anytime I wanted.

Now, I had to wake up, rub motherfuckin' lotion on. Something I'd never done in my entire life. Then slip the liner on over what remained of my leg, fit the pin in the socket of my prosthetic, then go about my day.

That wasn't the end of it, though.

There were days that I had to add extra socks to my leg because it shrinks. Then there are days I have to wear none at all because it's bloated.

I never realized just how much my legs changed throughout the day until I had to start fitting it into a piece of plastic that refused to bend, even a little bit.

I turned around and left, leaving Blake's concerned gaze at my back, passing the chief who was staring at his feet.

I would've escaped, too, as per my usual, but the minute I opened the door to leave, I ran into my over reacting brother.

"What's wrong?" He asked immediately.

I pushed past him. "I forgot my phone in the car. Is it alright if I go get it, mom?"

Mercy, my sister in law, snickered under her breath.

She was my partner in crime, helping me get away from Miller's concerned gaze watching my every move.

Sometimes I felt like I couldn't breathe…*like right now*.

The last thing I wanted was for the girl I had the hots for to look at me as less of a man. Which was what Blake had done. Regardless of whether she'd meant to or not.

***

"This is really good eating" Miller said, moaning over the taste of his lobster as he ate sloppily.

Luke, our captain on the SWAT team, snorted.

"Kinda hard to fuck up sea food, but it is pretty good. Missy did a fine good job," Luke said, dipping his piece of the tail into the butter with his fingers.

His wife, Reese, smacked him. "Use your fork, you Neanderthal."

He grinned, pieces of shellfish stuck to his teeth.

"That's nasty," Georgia said, grimacing.

Georgia was the wife to Nico, another member on the SWAT team. She was a sweet little thing that still amazed me, to this day, that she could handle the likes of her husband.

Nico was a dark son of a bitch. Always moody and rarely talking; he never seemed approachable.

Not that that bothered me. I could hold a conversation with him if I wanted to. I knew he'd have my back always, but I also knew he just wasn't that much of a talker, which suited me just fine. I didn't want to do much talking myself, lately.

"Blake made it," I said around a mouthful of French fries.

Luke looked at me sharply. "Blake?"

The Chief pointed to the back porch where Blake was currently sleeping on a hammock.

"My niece," he said.

I'd been wondering why she didn't eat, but I didn't want to let on that I cared.

So, I'd stayed silent and kept my eyes on her for the last two hours.

After she'd finished cooking, she'd slipped out the backdoor, and had laid down in the hammock. Then promptly fell asleep.

My eyes hadn't strayed from her form since.

She slept hard. It was almost as if she hadn't had any sleep since the bad call she'd taken three nights before.

Then to have her house broken into, on top of that, probably wasn't conducive to sleeping well at her own place.

"What's she doing out there?" Downy asked, turning around in his seat to look out the window. "She could've eaten with us."

"She has migraines," Chief Rhodes said. "Fresh air seems to help."

That explained the icepack.

It also explained why she was under a blanket in the shade, rather than in the sun.

I'd read somewhere that sun tended to have an adverse reaction to migraines.

"Eww," Memphis said. "You should tell her to look up pressure points

71

on the body. Those always used to help me."

"She doesn't have migraines anymore. I can hit one pressure point perfect…Owww! What'd you do that for?" Downy asked Memphis, rubbing the back of his arm where I'd guessed she'd pinched him.

She didn't even flinch from the big man's glare.

"Not at the dinner table, you big shit," Memphis glared.

I snorted, but nonetheless finished my lunch and stood. "It's been fun."

"You're leaving already?" Miller asked in surprise.

Before my accident, I'd been a social butterfly.

Now, though, not so much.

I'd rather be in my own company.

I literally did have somewhere to go, though.

"I have to get fitted for my new prosthesis. The blade," I said, finishing up my water and walking into the kitchen.

A couple of weeks ago, I'd been fitted for the blade, and today would be the first time I'd wear it.

Dumping my plate into the sink, I rinsed it off and then loaded it into the dishwasher.

As I was doing so, the backdoor opened.

I knew it was her without even turning around.

She smelled.

Not in a bad way, either.

That, at least, would make it a lot easier to deal with her. To get her out of my head.

But no. She had to smell like the goddamn sun in the middle of a rainstorm. The honeysuckles that bloomed wild around the county.

Jesus.

Small, nimble fingers emptied the ice pack I'd seen over her eyes earlier into the sink, and she walked to the side partially to toss the pack into a drawer filled with ones just like it.

"How was it?" She asked softly.

I put the fork into the washer and closed it before turning to her. "It was good."

She nodded, wincing slightly.

"Good," she said softly. "I'll see you later."

With that, she went out the garage door, to what I assumed was her car.

I watched her ass the entire way, too.

After saying my goodbyes, I walked out the front door and strode across the chief's lawn to my truck.

I had to pass Blake's car to get there, though, and that's when I saw her.

She was sitting in the front seat, crying.

I shook my head and kept walking.

I couldn't make myself get in, however.

I tried. I really did.

Valiantly, too.

But I was a sucker for crying women.

Just ask my mother and sister-in-laws.

Turning back, I walked to the car and tapped on her side window.

"You okay?" I asked warily.

She turned, rolling down her window, and the tears in her eyes nearly ripped my guts out.

"Yeah," she nodded, wiping her tears. "I just got a call that my house was broken into again."

She sniffled and wiped her hand across her face, wiping away the tears as best as she could without using a towel.

My stomach clenched. "Again, how do you know?"

She held up her phone up, and pressed play with her thumb.

"Blake, this is Janet Bowers with KPD. We've received another complaint that your front door was hanging open, and the neighbor suspected that someone was in there. Upon inspection, we found the place ransacked. We'd like you to come down to the station at your earliest convenience so we can file a report. We've locked your house back up, but since we were unable to get ahold of you, we'd like you to stop by."

Fuck.

"Get out, let's go," I said suddenly, startling her.

CHAPTER 9

*Remember, I'm a police officer. This story will need to have
dismemberment in it for me to be surprised.
-Foster to the rookie*

Foster

When she didn't move fast enough, I offered her my hand.

She looked up at me, startled, but nonetheless got out of her car, placing her soft hand inside my rough one.

My hand engulfed hers as I closed my fingers around it and started hauling her towards my truck.

It was my pride and joy.

I'd wanted the truck since I'd been old enough to dream about trucks.

It was a midnight blue extended cab Dodge diesel with thirty nine inch tires and an eight inch lift.

It sounded like a large cat purring when it started up, and still made me giddy when I first got in.

The comical part, though, was watching Blake climb in the passenger side.

In the end, I offered her a lift up.

My blood started to pump forcefully to parts that I didn't want it to be when my hands met the backs of her thighs, but I ignored it, and moved around to my side quickly.

The climb in was different with a prosthesis, but the concept was still the same. I just had to put all my weight on the real leg instead of the prosthesis. Something I'd had to learn to adapt to.

"Where are we going?" She asked quietly.

I started the truck, the rumbling purr vibrating my body softly.

"I have to go get fitted for my blade; but when I'm done, we're going to the station," I told her.

"Your blade? Like a new knife?" She asked worriedly.

I rolled my eyes, shooting her a peeved glance. "You don't get measured for a knife, darlin'. 'The Blade' is a type of running prosthesis. I'm getting fitted for it today. Actually, I've already been fitted. I'm getting it. I just hope it fits. It's uncomfortable as hell to run in the other one."

I pulled into Dr. Morton Stonewell's office twenty minutes later, and was sent straight back.

"Ahh," Dr. Stonewell said. "If it isn't my favorite patient."

I grimaced. "There's no reason to be so snotty."

Blake giggled, covering her mouth with her hand to cover up the faux pas.

Dr. Stonewell winked at Blake and patted the padded bench with his hand. "Hop up here, boy. Get that off, let's see what this fits like."

Dr. Stonewell went into his office, disappearing inside. I sat down, took off both shoes, and then stood up once again to shuck my pants off.

"Eeek!" Blake said, turning around quickly.

I chuckled as I pushed them down to my knees, exposing my boxer briefs. Taking a seat on the padded bench, I started to work the rest off my prosthesis.

No matter how hard I tried, it always turned out to be harder than it should be.

They got caught on everything on my prosthetic leg.

"Need help?" She asked softly.

I glared and she held her hands up.

"Geez, it just seems easier to use your hands instead of kicking your leg to get it off," she grumbled.

I barely stopped the smile that threatened to overtake my face.

So freakin' logical.

I got them off just as Dr. Stonewell poured out of his office, my new leg in his hand.

Blake's eyes widened as she saw it.

"That looks like a torture device," she gasped. "What's so special about it?"

"The Flex-Foot was designed to store kinetic energy. Almost like a spring does. It'll allow Foster to do whatever he wants to do. Run, jump, sprint, climb bleachers, pole vault. He can do whatever he wants to with this particular blade. If he can dream it, he can do it," Dr. Stonewell said animatedly.

I pressed the button at the base of my fake ankle, and pulled the old prosthetic off. Followed by the socks that filled in the prosthetic so I didn't bottom out in it.

Finally, off came my sleeve that held the pin on my leg with a sort of suction type sock.

I made sure to keep an eye on Blake, taking in her reaction as I did.

Maybe if I let her see what she'd really get with me, she'd get over whatever I saw in her eyes, lately, when I was around. As if I was the answer to her prayers.

I wasn't and she needed to know it.

"Wow," Blake said, dropping down to her haunches at my feet. "Can I touch it?"

She looked genuinely interested, so warily, I nodded. "Sure."

It felt weird, having her fingers running over my scar.

I didn't have much feeling at the bottom, where the scar was, but as she moved her fingers up to the sides, I could feel a lot more of her touch.

Why I'd get turned on by her rubbing her fingers on my stump, I didn't know, *but I did*.

Which was very awkward since I was currently sitting in my underwear.

"Does it hurt?" She asked.

Yes, my dick hurt. It was throbbing with need.

Moving quickly, I covered my crotch up with my pants and started rambling.

"It did hurt. Now, not so much unless I start having phantom pains," I said, quickly, to cover up the thoughts in my head.

"Alright, boy. Let's get this on."

***

An hour later had us walking into the police station, Blake slightly in front of me as we moved.

"Does it feel like you have kinetic energy stored in your foot?" She whispered loudly.

I barely contained the urge to snort at her question.

She was funny and I found that I didn't mind having her around as much as I thought I would.

She didn't bother me like my brothers. Or my parents. Or my friends.

I knew they were only concerned for me, but I was okay. I wasn't going to go into a deep depression, and I wasn't going to go off and flip a switch because I was missing a part of my body.

Sure, I was pissed, don't get me wrong, but I wasn't stupid.

I wasn't happy, per se, but I also wasn't bitter.

Mostly.

And Blake treated me like I was normal. She didn't react anything like I thought she would.

In fact, she acted like it wasn't even that big of a deal. She didn't flinch at the sight of my stump. She didn't look at me with pity. In fact, I was just Foster to her, and I liked that.

A lot.

"It feels weird. I'll have to go on a run later to try it out," I told her. "You wanna go?"

She looked over her shoulder at me, frowning.

"I don't think I could keep up with you. I run, but it's slower than molasses," she hedged.

I winked. "Don't worry. This might be one of those days that I run like that, too."

She pursed her lips, and nodded her head. "Okay. After we're done here and go check out my tainted house, then we can go."

I winced at how she said 'tainted.'

As if it was dirty.

Which I guess it was. At least to her.

"Where are you taking me?" She asked.

I nodded in the direction of the bullpen. "Detective Bower's desk is through there."

She nodded.

"Okay," she said. "You lead the way."

She grinned. "I just want to stare at your ass."

I winked at her and said, "It's a good ass. You'll never be able to look at another one the same way again."

As I said it, I drew the attention of a female officer at the water fountain as we moved.

She looked startled that I'd teased Blake.

Obviously, I was being somewhat surly lately. Something that probably wouldn't change anytime soon. Not unless Blake was around to pull out the nice in me, anyway.

I tossed a glare at the young officer as I passed, causing her to look down at her cup she'd been filling.

I hid the grin and continued to Bower's desk, stopping just to the right of the desk so Blake could take the only seat.

She'd stopped just to my right shoulder, hiding slightly behind me.

"What's up, Spurlock?" Bowers asked.

I reached for Blake's hand, and she moved her hands away so I couldn't grab them.

Instead, my hands met her belly, fingers brushing the soft skin of her abdomen.

Grabbing what I could, which happened to be the waistband of her pants, I pulled her until she moved reluctantly to my side.

I gave her a quick glance, and she was looking at anything other than the woman in front of her.

"How are you doing, Blake?" Detective Bowers asked, standing quickly.

Detective Bowers was a 10 year veteran on the force, and had just recently married another officer on the force.

She was okay, I guess, but she wasn't particularly my favorite person, either.

Which was also the case with Blake.

"Uhhh," Blake said dumbly. "Hi, Janet. How's it going?"

She smiled. "I'm really good, thank you for asking. How's life been?"

So Blake knew Janet. Interesting.

I made a mental note to ask her what the deal was when we got out of there.

"Oh, it's been going. You told us to come down here to file a report on my house?" Blake asked with a raised brow.

"Ohh! Yes!" Bowers said, sitting down. "I'm sorry, it's just been so long since I've seen you. I forget that you're here officially. Gosh, how long has it been?"

Blake ground her teeth.

I could hear it so well, in fact, that I had a feeling Bowers could hear it, too.

Moving my hand up to come to a rest on her hip, I gave her a reassuring squeeze, causing her to look at me quickly.

Her eyes were filled with annoyance and sadness, a double whammy of feelings that made me really feel for her.

Fucking David. He really knew how to fuck shit up.

He really had no clue what he was missing out on.

Oh, well. His loss was my gain, I supposed.

"Alright," Bowers said, pulling out some pictures. "Here is what we found when we went over there. There was some blood splatter near your bird cage. We took a sample of that, and we're going to have the crime techs analyze it. Hopefully there'll be a match when we run it through the system. The rest of the house was just tossed. Nothing broken, per se, but it's all out of place from what I could tell. The only other thing that I really saw that was bad, was the fact that they broke your door jam. David was sure to put up a board to cover your front door, though."

Blake tensed at the mention of David's name, but muttered, "Thank you," anyway.

"Am I allowed to stay there?" She asked softly.

Bowers nodded. "Of course," she said, standing up. "I'll just need you to sign this report detailing what I've told you, and warn you about the fact that, since this is the second incidence, there could be more to the story. Which was why I was given the case instead of just reporting it like what happened last time. Your uncle is aware of what happened as well."

Blake nodded. "Thanks."

"Hey, baby, are you almost done?" I heard called from my back.

Both Blake and I turned to see the male half of the relationship, Brandon Bowers, at our backs.

Brandon was the school resource officer for the area. From what I'd heard, he and Janet had been dating for some time before they'd finally tied the knot. Which also meant that they couldn't work anywhere near each other. Hence, why the former detective moved departments.

"Oh, hey! I haven't seen you in forever, Blake!" Brandon said, patting her shoulder.

He probably would've gone in for a hug, but Blake plastered herself to my side.

"Brandon," she nodded her head at him.

Brandon frowned at her, and pulled back. "How's it going?"

"Oh, not too bad. But we have to be going. Thank you for your help, Detective Bowers," Blake said hurriedly at my side, bending down to scribble her name on the paper in front of her.

"Oh," Janet said. "You changed your name back. I didn't realize."

Blake smiled sadly. "No, I'm sure you didn't."

With that, she took off, moving hurriedly through the room and out the door.

The last thing I saw before she rushed out the door was the tears in her eyes.

"What was that all about?" Brandon asked, sounding a little hurt.

I didn't bother to answer, following my charge as I hurried out the door behind Blake.

I found her leaning against my truck, her face buried in her hands and her shoulders shaking as she sobbed.

Something started to ache in my chest as I saw her distress.

"Blake," I rumbled softly once I reached her.

Placing both hands on either side of her head, I leaned down until I could hear what she was trying to say.

"They left me," she whispered, brokenly, through her sobs.

"Left you?" I asked, confused.

She nodded, turning around allowing me to see her face.

She nodded, gesturing towards the police station. "Those two. Hell, there're more. David screwed me over, and not one of them was there when I needed a friend the most. That's got to be what hurt the worst. David, I could deal with. But everyone left me, choosing him over me.

They all knew what he was doing. Every single one of them. I could see it on their faces the moment they realized that I knew. Pity. Sadness. Awareness. They apologized, but the damage was done. And not one of them *helped* me."

I pulled her into my arms, not able to stand the tears anymore. "It's okay, girly girl. They're not worth your time. If they're not there when you need them, they were never there to begin with. And I could tell you now that I know about eight men on the SWAT team that would willingly kick David's ass for you."

She giggled through her tears and wrapped her arms around my chest, relieving the ache that'd taken up a permanent home since I'd been with her.

"Thank you, Foster. You're a really great person. And I like your kinetic blade," she said softly.

"That sounds...*dirty*."

CHAPTER 10

I'm sorry I hurt your feelings. But it's not my fault you're stupid.
-Fact of life

Blake

"I hear you went out with a SWAT member. I thought you said you'd never date another cop as long as you lived," my mother said during lunch the next day. "Your father wants to meet him."

I'd talked her into going out, rather than her cooking something at their house.

I love my mom, but if I went to her house, then I'd be expected to stay longer than I really wanted to.

I knew she meant well, but I just couldn't handle her shit right now.

Especially when she got on the whole debate over David.

My mother was old fashioned.

She had that whole 'stand by your man' motto.

I, on the other hand, didn't have the 'stand by your man, even when he cheats' motto.

Something she couldn't fathom.

She was still upset that I'd left David.

She was raised to believe that women were made to please their man, and if they strayed, you were to turn a blind eye. Something I was never able to do.

She was really worried now that I'd be going to hell, too. Something that she made sure to mention.

"I didn't go out on a date. He helped me. That's all," I said around a mouthful of food.

My mother gave me a reproachful look. "Don't talk with your mouth full."

I raised my hands, chewed, and swallowed before I spoke next. "Sorry."

"You can bring him to dinner this Saturday. Your uncle and aunt will be there," she said, taking a bite of her own salad.

Yay. Sounded like an uber amount of fun.

Not.

I loved my mother and all, but there were times that the woman drove me batshit crazy.

My dad was probably insane just by having to listen to us go at it so often.

"We'll see," I said before taking another bite. "He works, you know. And he's not my boyfriend; he has no obligation to come."

"Uh-huh. I saw David shopping with his fiancé this morning. You didn't tell me they were expecting a baby," my mother admonished.

The salad started to turn to acid in my stomach as I thought about, yet again, how much David had screwed me over. Even my own mother liked him better. Which I guess was okay since David's father liked *me* better. It was only fair.

Only David's father was dead, and my mother was still very much alive. And still loved David like he was her own.

I ignored her, hoping she'd give it up, but she didn't. She never could leave well enough alone.

She was the match to my gasoline. She knew how to light me up better than anybody, and she proved it with her next comment.

"I can't wait to see if it's a boy or a girl. I've been waiting so long for a grandchild," she whispered happily.

I froze with the salad halfway to my mouth, looking at her incredulity. "You're fucking kidding me right now, aren't you?"

She tilted her head slightly. "Kidding you about what?"

"You can't wait to have a fucking grandchild?" I whispered deceptively calm.

"Watch your language," she said reproachfully, looking around at all of the people around us.

I could give less than a fuck what they thought.

"Do you realize that David had a fucking girlfriend for two motherfuckin' years?" I asked, my voice raising an octave. "Or how about the fact that he never told me he was fucking someone else. The least he could have done was use a goddamned condom around us. But no, not David fucking Dewitt. He was too goddamned special. He could do no fucking wrong. But you wouldn't know how that feels, because my daddy is the best of the best. He's so fucking awesome that you'll never have to experience how that feels. Me, not so lucky. Now I get to watch while some bitch gets to have my life. Now, for the first time in nearly three and a half years, I'm starting to feel *happy* again, and you have to pull this bullshit. I lost everything. My friends. My husband. My mother. Daddy, Uncle Darren and Aunt Missy are the only people in my life that have helped me, until recently. Now, I'd appreciate it if you never brought up David again. Because, let's just say, the sound of his name makes me want to vomit the last five years of food I've eaten into his face."

With that, I threw down a crumpled twenty from my pocket, tossed my napkin over my plate, and stormed out of the restaurant.

My eyes landed on David in the fucking corner, and a smile touched my lips. Good, the fucker deserved to hear that. So did his shit head of a fiancé.

My only hope was that she put the baby they were having up for adoption. That poor kid didn't deserved to have those two assholes as parents.

That's when I saw *him*.

Foster.

He had a smile tilting up the corner of his lips, and his eyes were alight with mirth as he watched me walk towards him.

He was near to laughing, in fact.

"What are you laughing at?" I snapped as I stormed past him.

He trailed behind me, leaving his brother and a blonde giant behind.

Both of their eyes were on us as I pushed out the door.

"Who's the Viking?" I asked over my shoulder.

Today, Foster was wearing his work uniform. He had on his new blade instead of the other prosthesis, and he seemed almost…happier.

His eyes were crinkled at the corners as he smiled full out at me. The first real smile I'd ever seen him do.

"That's Luke, my boss," he said, walking with me.

He didn't even have a limp anymore.

"You look like you have a spring in your step," I said warily.

He gave me a droll look.

"Really, how original," he said dryly.

I stuck my tongue out at him. "For real, though. You look better than

I've ever seen you."

He shrugged. "It always makes me happy to see a woman stick it to her ex. Something you really did. I don't think you know it, but the entire SWAT team, as well as the big bosses, and a few of the other cities SWAT teams, were sitting in that room just behind you. I'd gone out to show the rest of ours where we were."

My mouth dropped open. "You're shitting me."

He shook his head. "No. And trust me, every one of them heard you. Their eyes were already on you to begin with. They heard every word."

I stopped and turned towards him.

He didn't stop, though, and ran into me.

"Shit," he said, grabbing me to him before I could fall from the force.

Our bodies were pressed against each other's from chest to thigh and, before I knew it, his mouth was on mine.

We were a lot closer to my car than I realized, because suddenly my back was pressed against the warm metal with Foster's large body.

I moaned into his mouth, gasping as he dug something massive into my pubic bone.

His tongue tangled with mine and his hands found my hair as he pushed into me, swiveling his hips as he did.

When he finally disengaged his mouth from mine, I looked up at him with a dazed expression. His brown eyes looking full of need. "I like you, Blake."

I blinked. "I like you, too."

"You're not alone. I'm here. Even if I'm not a very nice person to talk to all the time, I'm fucking here."

I nodded. "Okay."

"Just don't forget it, okay?"

I nodded. "Yeah, okay."

As I got into my little car and pulled out of the parking lot, I looked back at him standing there.

His eyes watched me. As if he were stalking his prey. Surveying it to make sure I did what he expected it to do.

I must've done it, too, because he smiled.

Widely.

Full out.

All encompassing.

And my lips weren't the only thing tingling.

CHAPTER 11

Do you want the rest of my cake?
-Said no one ever

Blake

"Yes?" I asked to the two men at my front door.

They were massive. And when I say massive, I mean humongous. Fucking huge.

Huger than huge.

Muscled. Ripped. Jacked. Those were only a few words that I'd use to describe them.

Oh, and they were hot, too.

One had dark hair, tanned skin, and if I had to guess, some sort of Puerto Rican background. I used to have a friend that had the same dark hair and beautiful skin.

His eyes were a deep shade of brown, and looked nearly black in his face.

The other man was easily just as big, but he had caramel colored hair and green eyes. What really set him apart, though, was the scar that ran down his face.

They also rode motorcycles.

I'd heard those first.

Which was what enabled me to watch as they'd dismounted, and then walked up my front walk while talking.

I wasn't scared, though.

Foster had warned me with a note slapped to my front door, after I got back from my run, that they'd be here.

If I hadn't been warned it would've been a different story.

"We're here to set up an alarm for you," the darker of the two rumbled.

I swallowed. "I didn't order an alarm."

I hadn't seen that on the note. It'd said that he had a couple of friends coming over later in the day to take a look at my locks. It had said nothing about an alarm.

That cheeky bastard. He had to have known that I wouldn't have allowed them to come over and do that.

Stuff like that cost money. Money which I didn't have just floating around.

I made just enough in a week to cover my bills, groceries, and a few frivolous things. Not something expensive like an alarm system.

"I don't have the money to pay for that. I'm sorry you wasted your trip," I told them honestly.

They exchanged glances with each other.

It was the smirk on both of their lips that had my back feathers ruffling.

"Foster said you'd say that. You need to just let us do our job. Apparently, it was funded by the police department," Scarface said. "My name is Max."

He held out his hand to me, and I took it, shaking it.

I must've surprised him with the force I put into it, because he squeezed my hand a little harder before he released me.

"Gabe," tall, dark and dangerous said, offering me his hand.

I took his as well, and stepped out of the doorway, allowing them in.

"Well," I didn't really know what to say. "Do you need me for anything?"

"Only access to the house. Which you've already done. Later, we'll need more guiding on the code. So be thinking of something easy you want to use. A six digit number is best. Nothing consecutive," Max told me.

I nodded and swept my arm in an arc.

But I stopped them before they could get more than two feet.

"Do either of you have Foster's number?" I asked hopefully.

They smiled.

"No, pretty lady. We don't."

With that comment, they left.

Stubborn men.

I damn well knew that they had his number.

They had to.

Foster had asked them not to give it to me, though.

I knew it just as well as I knew that the police department wasn't the one paying for it, he was.

A smile kicked up the corner of my lip, and I closed my eyes.

What was the feeling in my chest?

After an hour of watching The Price is Right, I decided I knew what it was.

Excitement. I was actually looking forward to something for the first time in a very long time.

And it was a fight.

Hopefully a fight that would lead to something…more.

***

I was painting my toes when what sounded like a movie started to play at full blast.

It played out just like an action movie. The part where a hail of gunfire starts peppering the surroundings, and the people all hide behind the car and miraculously don't get hit.

My head peaked up from its hunched position over my toes, and surveyed the area.

I hadn't even heard them move.

It was like they were trained in the art of ninja or something.

One second they were nowhere to be seen, and the next I was being hauled backwards.

I spilled my nail polish in the process, and all I could focus on, while a tattooed, muscled forearm belonging to Max, hauled me back, was the fact that the spilled polish resembled a pool of blood.

"What the fuck?" Max barked in frustration when he saw my side room.

They hadn't had a chance to get to that room, obviously.

It was filled to the brim with books.

The entire four walls were packed three feet high and three paperbacks thick.

Nonetheless, Max dropped us down to the floor and covered me with his body.

This wasn't anywhere near as erotic as I'd imagined it being

Firstly, in my books, the heroine was always in love with the one protecting her.

Secondly, the man at my back was married, and I couldn't feel that way about someone that was married.

He'd been talking about his wife, Peyton, for a good hour and a half now, and frankly I was a little jealous.

I wanted what she had.

But I was also happy for her. It was nice that someone had the devotion of a man like Max.

Someone that would protect her like the way he was doing to me, with his life.

Sure, he'd do it for stranger, too, which he was exhibiting now. But it wouldn't be that blind devotion that he'd give to his wife.

The shooting, which had continued this entire time, suddenly stopped.

My ears rang in the silence, and I finally took my first breath in three minutes.

Well, I'd probably taken others, but I wasn't counting those. Those were panic breaths.

Max's heavy body didn't move, and I laid there, wondering when he would.

"Are you going to get off of me?" I asked after a while longer.

"Shh," he hissed.

That's when I noticed that the other man, Gabe, wasn't with us.

What if that man died?

He had a wife.

And kids.

Oh, my God. *It'd be all my fault!*

The sound of Gabe's voice from somewhere beyond had me breathing a sigh of relief.

Max finally got off of me, and hauled me effortlessly to my feet.

Then he proceeded to drag me into the living room, giving me the first good look at my house. And I realized just how close I came.

"Well," I said breathlessly. "I don't think there's any point in installing that alarm."

I'd said that, though, because of the fact that my living room wall resembled Swiss cheese.

"Jesus," I breathed.

Then I turned my head to watch as Gabe entered the room, blood streaming down his arm.

"You've been shot!" I wailed in despair.

***

"Gabe!" A woman's frantic voice wailed from the doorway.

I turned to see a beautiful blonde dart across the room, and throw herself into Gabe's arms.

I got up quietly, exiting the room as the couple embraced.

We'd gotten to the hospital less than twenty minutes ago, and I'd sat with Gabe while a doctor looked at the bullet hole on his arm. Something he called a 'graze.'

I called it a fucking bullet hole, but who the heck was I to say any differently?

"Blake!" My ex-husband's voice called loudly from the entrance.

I looked up at him and glared.

Why was he here?

"Are you okay?" David asked, hurrying up to me.

I nodded.

"What's going on?" David wondered, taking a step forward as if to pull me into his arms.

I shrank away from him, flinching back out of his reach.

He didn't get the privilege to touch me. Not anymore.

"Blake!" A deep, frantic voice said before a hard body snatched me up.

My eyes started to water, and I wrapped my arms firmly around Foster's muscled chest.

His heart was beating frantically against my ribs, and the tears that I'd been keeping at bay by sheer force of will finally broke free.

I cried into his shirt. *Hard.*

I wasn't a very attractive crier.

My eyes got puffy and red, my nose ran, and my face scrunched up into a mass of quivering goo.

Foster didn't care what I looked like, though.

He still held me firmly to his chest, rocking me back and forth.

His fingers threaded into the knot I had at the top of my head, working the mass of my hair loose.

He threaded his fingers through it, and held my head in the palm of his hand.

"Are you okay?" He asked after a while.

I nodded. "I'm okay."

"Your ex-husband looks like he wants to geld me," he rumbled.

"My ex-husband is a douche canoe," I told him honestly.

He snorted. "Possibly."

"How'd you know I was here?" I asked, leaning my head back so I could see his face.

He raised his eyebrow as if to ask, 'really?'

I smiled.

Clarifying, I said, "What I meant, was that I thought you were out of town today. That's what your note said."

He winked. "I know what you meant. I wasn't far out of town, though. Just at some continuing education. They were more than willing to let me go when they realized that my girl had her house shot up like a tin can at target practice."

My mouth gaped open.

"Your girl?" I gasped.

He raised that annoying eyebrow again.

"I decided," he confirmed.

"You decided?" I asked, outrage starting to leak into my voice.

I, of course, wasn't that upset about his high handedness.

I was surprised, though.

He hadn't even given me the first inkling other than that kiss last night that he was even interested.

Then all of a sudden I was his girl?

"If I gave you the choice you'd have to think about it. And I didn't want that mind of yours to start thinking, so I just made it myself," he said bluntly.

I just shook my head, not knowing what to say.

I was excited, though.

Butterflies were roiling in my belly as I said, "We'll see."

He shook his head. "No, we won't."

"Yes, we will."

"Won't."

"Will!"

He raised that stupid brow again, and pulled me close again before placing a soft kiss on my cheek. "Won't."

"Blake?" My father's worried voice called from behind me.

I turned in Foster's arms, arms that he dropped, allowing me to move away from him slightly to see my father's worried face.

"Daddy," I said, walking towards him.

He gathered me into his arms, dropping his chin onto the top of my head as he said, "You scared the shit out of me, girl."

I squeezed him tightly, feeling the familiar feeling of his Kevlar vest digging into my cheek as I did. "I'm okay."

His body shook as he started to cry and I felt horrible.

My daddy was a big man. A bad ass man.

But I was also his little girl. His only child. His pride and joy.

It probably tore him apart to hear that my house had been the location of a drive by shooting. *With me inside.*

"Who's the man?" He asked.

I turned to see Foster across the room, talking quietly with my uncle, Gabe, and Max.

My uncle had been the first to arrive.

I'd gotten the same reception from him.

"That's…" Foster? That didn't sound like enough for him. Hero. The man I'm falling for. The sexiest man in Kilgore, Texas. Those sounded better, yet I knew my dad probably wouldn't find the same humor I did in it. "That's Foster."

"That the man your mother and you got in a fight about?" He asked, rubbing his stubble across the top of my head.

I smiled. "He was what started it, yes."

"Hmm," he hummed. "He coming over for dinner tonight?"

I glanced up at Foster, seeing his eyes on me, and smiled. "Why don't you ask him?"

I actually got a little giddy inside when he did just that, walking right up to Foster, and offering him his hand.

"You the one who had men at her apartment today?" Dad asked bluntly.

Foster nodded. "This is Max," he gestured with his hand. Then said, "And this is Gabe. They're with Free."

My dad shook both man's proffered hands, and said, "Come to dinner. It's at one. Both of you, too. Bring the family."

With that, he gave my uncle a look, and started to walk away.

Uncle Darren followed, shooting me an exasperated look.

Daddy was older than Uncle Darren by five years.

He was a certified bad ass, and everybody who was anybody knew my dad. Uncle Darren was, and always would be, Shank's brother.

Daddy's real name was Louis, but when he first started out, he was pulling double shifts. One as a trooper, and another as a prison guard at Huntsville State Penitentiary.

When he was on duty at Huntsville, an inmate made a shank out of a toothbrush, sharpening the end into a lethal point.

Then made an arrow out of it, wrapping wet newspaper and who knew what else into it, honing it into a lethal weapon.

Then, as my father passed by one night, the prisoner had used the elastic from his shorts, tied it to the bars, and then launched the arrow at my father.

It hit my father in the throat barely missing his carotid artery by a scant millimeters.

Daddy had gotten that taken care of at the infirmary, and then finished his job.

Only when he was done at work did he go to see his doctor, who told him he was a very lucky man, and that as long as he kept the wound clean, he could return to work.

Although painful, it was nothing but a minor wound that could've been deadly.

So he went about working, never letting that phase him.

The nickname stuck, and Uncle Darren was forever going to be remembered as Shank's little brother, no matter what his accolades were.

"Was that Shank Rhodes?" Gabe whispered loudly. "You're related to Shank Rhodes?"

I blinked, turning to look at Gabe. "Yeah, why?"

"Oh, fuck," Max and Foster said at the same time.

I really started to get confused then.

"What?" I asked, voice rising.

Which caught the attention of Gabe's wife, Ember, who'd been speaking with an ER nurse. She walked up and wrapped her arms around Gabe from behind, poking her eyes out to see around his large arm.

Gabe wrapped his good arm around Ember's back, holding her close as he said, "Somebody just shot up Shank's kid's house. Oh, my fucking God."

Foster's eyes widened, and he wrapped his arm around me.

"Mother fucker," he breathed.

Ember, who'd stayed silent since she'd arrived, stared at me, taking in Foster's arm placement, and then held out her hand to me.

"My name's Ember, it's nice to meet you," Ember said pleasantly.

I took her hand, and shook it. "It's nice to meet you, too. My name's Blake Rhodes."

"You're Officer Shank's kid?" She asked, eyes widening slightly.

I threw my hands up in annoyance. "What's the big fucking deal with that?"

They all started talking at once, as if they were all little kids scared of the big bad school yard bully.

"He's a badass."

"You do not mess with The Shank."

"The Shank is a fucking legend."

"I heard about him while I was in Las Vegas."

I just shook my head. "So should I ask him about this, or are you all going to give me the details that I need to make an informed decision?"

They stayed silent.

Obviously they'd rather stay silent.

Perfect.

CHAPTER 12

9 out of 10 children get their awesomeness from their father.
-Proven fact

Foster

"Look at her fucking house," Luke said, shaking his head in flabbergasted silence.

It was bad.

Really bad.

The entire house was ruined.

The front wall of the house, where the brick had once been, was nothing more than a mess of rubble.

In some places, you could see through the walls in a three feet wide mass.

"Dude, you're dating Shank's daughter?" Downy yelled, announcing his arrival with that big mouth of his.

I turned, catching my good foot on a stray brick, and tripped.

"Fuck," I said, catching myself.

"Hey, that was pretty cool," Downy said, looking down at my 'blade.'

I found that I liked it.

It didn't look remotely like a foot, like the other one did, but it was more functional…at least for me.

Everyone knew I was an amputee, anyway, so what was the point of hiding that fact?

"Yeah," I said, bouncing lightly on the blade. "It's pretty cool. As for doing anything with The Shank's daughter, I won't be speaking to you, or anyone, about that."

"Good," a dark, menacing voice said from behind me.

I turned to see Officer Shank, himself, inspecting the lot of us.

Gabe and Max were still with us, and they'd been joined by the rest of the SWAT team: Downy, Luke, Nico, Bennett, Michael, Miller, John, and James.

When something happened to one, something happened to all. And, although I hadn't started anything 'official' with Blake, they knew she was mine.

Just as much as Shank knew it, too. That'd been why he invited me to dinner.

Downy, who'd been the one to make the comment about Blake, blushed.

Fucking blushed.

Downy was a talker. He never knew when to shut up, but anyone with any sense at all knew better than to talk shit about The Shank. Even Downy.

"Sir," I said, offering my hand.

He shook it, then surprised me by pulling me into a hug.

"I know you weren't here, but you put into motion having *them* here. If you ever, and I mean ever, need anything, call me. I'll be there. You saved my girl's life," he said lowly, just loud enough for me, and me only, to hear. "Oh, and call me Lou. That Shank shit is getting old."

I swallowed and slapped him on the back before he let me go.

I was actually a little choked up.

Getting a favor owed to me by The Shank, *Lou*, was big. Fucking monumental.

"You can all come to dinner," Lou said before he nodded at us, and then walked down the street.

"Holy fucking shit," Downy breathed.

I raised my brow at them. "I'm man-crushing."

They all snorted. Every last one of them.

"And you're dating his daughter. If you ever fuck up, you're dead," Miller announced.

That wasn't something that hadn't crossed my mind. More than once, in fact.

It was bad enough that she was the Chief of Police's niece. Now she had to be The Shank's daughter, too.

Knowing Blake's father was The Shank wouldn't change my mind about Blake though.

"Do you know that he has the record for the most drug related arrests in the state?" Luke asked the group as a whole.

"He also has the most weapon draws," I countered.

"The most officer involved shootings," Max rumbled.

I winced.

"The most…"

I ignored the rest of the comments, going off to walk around the rest of the house.

Once I got my fill of the outside, I walked inside, taking in the destruction.

The bullets had torn through the first two walls.

There were even some in the kitchen.

My mind struck on the spilled red nail polish on the coffee table.

Bullets riddled the floor, couch, and area surrounding the couch.

Red nail polish was spilled carelessly all over the floor, the bright red sight making bile rise in my throat.

That very well could've been her blood.

She could've died.

She would've died had Max and Gabe not been there.

"Did you get the plate numbers?" I asked Gabe.

I'd heard him come in behind me, taking in the destruction alongside me.

"Yeah, the plates were stolen. I have Jack doing what he can from the computer end, though," Gabe said powerlessly.

Jack was another member of Free, and a computer wizard.

He was extremely smart, and from what I'd heard, his wife was even smarter.

The two of them together were a fucking wet dream in the hacker world.

And it made me happy to know they were on my side for this.

"Thank you," I replied just as softly.

"There were two of them. That I know," Gabe offered.

I nodded my head. "I should've gotten you out here the day before yesterday. Goddammit, then we would've had cameras up."

"No," my brother said from the doorway. "Then you would've just had a dead Blake. Sure, you would've known, maybe, who it was, but you wouldn't have any reason to know anymore, other than vengeance."

My older brother and his fucking logic sometimes made a lot of sense.

"Yeah," I agreed. "Not sure there's any reason to put cameras up anymore. But we're going to anyway. And I need Mercy's men to come out and start working on her house."

Miller nodded. "Mercy's already started on it."

Did I say I really loved my sister in law?

"Thanks," I said, continuing to walk through the room over to the area where Max had taken her during the shooting.

I blinked in surprise when I saw the millions of freakin' books lining the walls.

There had to be at least a small fortune's worth.

"So, she's a reader?" Miller asked, picking up a book that'd fallen from its shelf.

I took the book from him, smiling when I saw a highlander on the cover wearing nothing but a kilt.

"Looks like it," I said. "Nothing better to do but fantasize, I suppose. Collect books of all the men she wished her ex-husband would've been."

"Speaking of ex," Michael said from the doorway. "He's here."

I liked Michael, although I didn't know him as well as the others.

I'd been on the SWAT team for a little over two years now, and I felt like I knew just about as much about him now as I had when I first started working with him.

I knew he'd have my back if I needed help, but aside from our work relationship, I didn't know much more about him.

I was fairly sure, though, that the tattoos covering his body told some sort of story.

They fairly had to with the sheer amount of them he had.

"Thanks," I said, patting his shoulder as I passed him.

He grunted.

I found David on the front lawn, studying the destruction.

"'Sup?" I muttered.

I didn't really care for David before, but now I *really* didn't care for him.

He was an ass, and to know he treated Blake like shit only accentuated the fact that he was a douchebag.

"I wanted to come over here and offer Blake a place to stay, but the tattooed one said she wasn't here," David said, eyes roaming the pile of rubble.

I snorted. "With who? Your new woman? Or other woman?"

He glared. "Yeah, what's it to you?"

I smiled. "I'm sure she'd rather have died in the drive-by today than stay at that house with you and the woman you cheated on her with. I'll be sure to mention it later, when she's at my place, that you offered, though."

He started forward, but stopped himself with only a step in my direction. "You need to stay away from her."

I raised a brow at him, giving him a mocking smile. "Oh yeah? And who are you to question me?"

He raised his lip in a snarl. "You're nothing but a washed up gimp who can't fucking do anything, but gets special treatment because he was one of the select few on the SWAT team. You're only on there still because they can't legally fire you."

I heard a snort behind me, but didn't turn around.

"Is that what you think?" I asked slowly.

He shrugged. "I don't think. I know."

"You think you can get onto the SWAT team? Do what we do?" I taunted him.

"I fucking know I can. I just have a wife at home to worry about," he shot back.

I laughed then.

"A wife that you cheated on your original wife with?" Blake hissed. "You're such a crock of shit. Should I tell them that you wear a fucking girdle under your uniform to hold your gut in?"

I turned to see her walking down the street towards us.

I'd missed her. Even that sneer that was currently directed at her ex.

She'd said that she was going to come by, but I'd expected her to drive, not walk.

Apparently, I needed to pay a little more attention and explain to her that she couldn't be doing that anymore.

I didn't want her to be out running without protection of some kind. Hell, right now she didn't need to be out, *period*.

"Get the fuck away from my house, David," she snapped.

"I paid for that house!" David growled.

"Yeah, you did, didn't you? But you know what? So did I. Remember when we got married and you said what's yours was mine? Well, there you go. I deserved the fucking money to buy this house. And I also deserve the settlement I got," she spat. "Get the fuck over it."

"Well, it's only for another six months. Hope you have your shit in order, because after that day, you won't be getting another fucking dime from me," he yelled before turning on his heel and stomping back to his truck.

"I freakin' hate that man," she growled as she watched him walk away.

I turned to her, pulling her into my arms. "I do, too."

She smiled, leaning her head back to look at me. "That made me totally hot, seeing you taunting him."

I grinned. "How hot?"

She blinked, all signs of teasing gone. "Hot enough that if we were alone right now, I'd show you."

"Hot damn," Downy yelled. "I need to get home to my wife! See y'all at dinner!"

Blake's face flushed as she watched Downy walk away.

"That was embarrassing," she admitted, burying her face into my shoulder.

I laughed, but something silver caught my eye as Downy pulled his car away.

A woman sat in her car across the street.

She'd been hidden by Downy's huge truck, but now that he was gone, I could clearly see her sitting there.

She stared right at me for long seconds before she, too, started her car and drove away.

"What?" Blake asked, startling me.

I memorized the license plate number, before replying. "Nothing. It was nothing. And don't let Downy embarrass you. He's got a mouth, but he won't make a big deal of anything that goes on between us."

She smiled, looking relieved, and said, "Good."

"Now," I said, leading her to my truck. "About being alone…"

CHAPTER 13

Everyone loves my cooking. Even the smoke alarm cheers me on.
-Kitchen sign

Blake

"Are you sure you want me to stay here?" I asked, looking around at the apartment.

"I haven't stayed here in weeks since this," Foster said, gesturing to his leg. "But it's got clean sheets, thanks to Mercy. And I'm going to stay here with you until we figure out why you have people breaking into, and shooting up, your house," Foster replied as he dropped his keys onto the coffee table.

"Has it been empty?" I asked, looking around at the ultimate bachelor pad.

There wasn't much to it. From what I could see, there were two bedrooms. One was empty but for a bed and a dresser, the other was empty but for a bed.

The living room was much the same, only sporting an older TV, two couches that looked to be purchased from a yard sale, and a table in between the kitchen and the living room, sans chairs.

"Is there anything you need or want from the house…something you can't live without?" Foster asked. "They'll have your front wall replaced by the end of the week, and the rest fixed in no more than three weeks. It shouldn't take you long to get back there…if that's what you want."

I opened my mouth, hesitant to say it. "Umm, it's heavy."

"What is?" he asked, dropping his arm full of bags onto the table and turning back to me.

I worked my lip between my teeth, finally deciding to just say it.

"My pottery wheel."

He blinked. "Pottery wheel?"

I nodded. "Yeah, my pottery wheel. I dug it out of storage when I left David, and well…I like it. It helps me sleep."

"Is this like one of those things that you can make big mounds of dirt into a bowl?" He asked, eyebrows drawing down in concentration.

I nodded. "Clay. But yes, one and the same."

"Isn't something like that dirty?" He asked, walking into the kitchen and pulling a beer from the fridge.

The house was completely empty except for beer in the fridge. Now *that* was the ultimate bachelor pad.

"It can be dirty, yes. But I have plastic underneath the one in my house. I just mop the floor when I'm done," I said. "My kiln is outside my house. I won't need to use that until I have about ten pots ready to fire, so I don't need it here."

He nodded. "Where would be best for you to set it up?"

I went into the bedrooms.

Noticing that the spare bedroom didn't have a bathroom I said, "I can do it in that room, it'd just be easier if I had it near a water source."

He nodded. "How big is it?"

I held my hands as wide as I could get them. "This wide."

He shook his head. "I'll measure it. We'll figure it out. Sounds to me like it'd be easier to just do it right here."

He pointed to the corner of the living room, which happened to be nearest the bathroom.

"The rooms are too small to hold much more than a dresser and a bed. If you put it in there you're going to have too much shit everywhere. At least here you can do it without it being in the way," he observed, tilting the beer up to his lips.

"Thank you," I said seriously. "That really means a lot to me."

He shrugged. "As long as you don't care that I sleep with all the TV's on, we'll be okay. I can't stand the constant quiet."

I nodded.

"That's fine," I said, nerves starting to take over when I realized that we'd be staying in the same place for over three weeks.

Three weeks of being in close quarters with a man that set fire to my blood, and stirred things in me that hadn't been stirred in a very, *very* long time.

"We'll get your wheel after dinner. Are you ready? Do you need to change?" He asked hopefully.

I looked down at my blue jean shorts, yellow flip flops, and lime green halter top. "What's wrong with what I have on?"

He swallowed. "Your breasts. I can see them."

I looked down, and sure enough, I could see them too. "What's the big deal?"

"I've been trying to ignore the fact that you can see your nipples through the shirt," he said, walking forward slowly as if not to spook me. "But I can't."

Little did he know that it took a lot to spook me. Such as a freakin' thunderstorm, and I was fairly sure Foster was nothing more than a little thunder cloud.

I might get a little rumble of thunder from him with his constant need to protect and serve, regardless of who it was, but it'd never be anything more than that.

Then thunderstorms were the last thing on my mind as his long, blunt finger, circled the tip of my nipple.

I gasped as the feeling shot straight through to my toes.

My breasts had always been sensitive. Something that David never tried to explore.

I'd asked him, again and again, to touch my breasts, to suck on them, but he'd always steered clear of them.

I'd thought something was wrong with them, but suddenly I knew I was wrong.

Especially when Foster yanked my shirt to the side, allowing my breast to pop free of the built in bra and bounce with his exuberance.

He leaned down, and roughly captured my nipple into his mouth, sucking hard.

Hard enough that I clenched my core tightly. My pussy closing in on itself, desperate for something to be inside of it.

Anything!

He read me like an open book, though.

Letting his hand sneak around the back of my short shorts, he slipped two long fingers up and inside. Gliding underneath the elastic of my thong and delving in between my folds in a matter of seconds.

My eyes closed on their own volition, which was why I was surprised when he bit down on my nipple, causing me to gasp in excitement.

Then, finally, his fingers found my pussy and plunged inside.

Filling me completely…*with only two fingers.*

More than I'd ever been filled before, and I didn't even have the real thing yet.

"God," I breathed, eyes slamming open in surprise when he sucked hard on my nipple once again.

I looked down, watching his strong, bristly jaw work as he sucked powerfully, drawing my nipple deeply into his mouth.

My hand moved down to cup the back of his head with both hands as I went up onto my tiptoes and circled my hips, searching for something.

More friction, possibly.

Yet again, though, he knew what I wanted.

Thrusting his fingers in and out of me at a furious pace, curling in to work that special spot inside of me.

Then his voice, his goddamned voice, was what made me explode.

That sexy, deep baritone whispering all the dirty things he'd been wanting to do to me since he'd met me, made me come. And come so hard I screamed.

It took me a few long seconds to come back to my senses, but when I did, and opened my eyes, it was to find his intense ones staring back at me.

"You're so fucking sexy," he said, pulling his fingers from my pussy, then promptly sucking them clean with his mouth.

I gaped at him, stunned with how he could go from zero to ninety in point three seconds.

Letting me go carefully, he stepped back and readjusted himself.

I smiled, reaching for his belt, but he stopped me.

My heart, which had been frantically beating against my ribcage, froze for a few short moments.

"There's not enough time in the world to do what I want to do to you," he said, softening the blow.

When I moved to head to the bathroom to clean the flood between my legs up, he grabbed my hands and stopped me.

"Don't," he said simply.

I raised my brows at him. "Why?"

He grinned as he said, "You're gonna need that later. And it won't be the last time I do that tonight before we actually get to the main event. The buildup is going to drive you fucking crazy, but I promise it'll be worth it."

With that lovely parting comment, he slapped me on my ass, sending me on my way.

***

I was nervous.

I knew tonight would be the night.

The night I had sex with the second person in my life.

The second person that could make or break what I thought sex could be.

With David, it'd always been bland.

Towards the end of our relationship, it'd turned into an every Thursday kind of thing.

With Foster, though, I had a feeling that it'd be spontaneous. And hot.

Really hot.

"Why are you biting your fingernails?" Foster asked

"You're about to meet my mother," I lied.

He snorted. "You need to be careful when you lie. You have a tell," he laughed.

I blinked, and turned in my seat to face him.

"What tell?" I asked him.

He pointed to my lip that I was currently worrying with my teeth, and I winced.

Yeah, I did do that. Often.

It was a nervous habit. Something I did a lot, I'd found.

"I'll have to see what I can do about remedying that," I teased.

He winked and bailed out of the truck with a bounce in his step that had nothing to do with the kinetic energy stored in his prosthesis.

He moved around his truck, walked up to my door, and opened it.

Offering me his hand, he helped me down and held it as he slammed the door behind me.

I walked with him, in silence, up to the door.

We stopped once we reached the front door, though.

That was because we heard fighting.

Well, my mother was yelling, and my father did what he did best, ignored her.

I wasn't really sure that my parents loved each other.

In fact, there were days that I was fairly sure they hated each other.

The only thing that I thought kept them together was that they'd been together so long they didn't know any different.

I'd asked my dad why he didn't divorce, and he'd said that it wasn't 'his way.'

He'd never leave my mother.

End of story.

But as I stood there on the front steps of my parents' home, I knew that they were through.

"Choose!" My mother screeched.

My father's deep, calm voice said. "Don't make me do that. You know what I'll choose."

My mother's voice became shrill. "You have to choose! I won't allow you to let her treat me like that! You've been avoiding this for days. If you don't say what you choose, right now, then I'll only assume I know what you're picking and act accordingly."

"You walk out this door, I won't let you back in."

Then, she did just that.

She opened the side door, stormed out to her minivan, and peeled out of the driveway, narrowly missing Foster's truck by a hair's width.

I walked into the front door, seeing my father and grandfather on the couch, both with a beer in their hand.

My father looked pissed, and my grandfather looked tired.

"So…" I said, catching their attention. "Are we ordering pizza?"

I couldn't say that I was upset about my mother leaving.

We'd never really gotten along.

She continued, to this day, to try to mold me into the perfect housewife. Something that I really, really didn't want to be.

She hated that I did pottery.

She hated that I left David.

She hated that I didn't wear my hair down, or put on dresses that 'flattered my figure.'

Personally, I couldn't give a fuck about all of that. What I wanted to do was what I loved, and being the 'perfect housewife', like she was, wasn't one of them.

And color me surprised when she'd made that ultimatum to my father.

That was something I'd never thought to hear uttered from her lips.

"You can go finish making the dinner that your mother left cooking on the stove," Grandpa said, eyes never leaving the TV.

It was on a fishing show.

He loved fishing shows.

I loved them, too, which was why I made a note of the channel before I went into the kitchen.

Then I turned it on and finished making dinner.

My mom had chosen fried chicken, mashed potatoes, and fresh baked rolls.

I was okay with the first two, but the last never turned out how I wanted it to.

It never failed. My bread was always too thick. On the verge of being brick-like thick.

Bread machine. By hand and baking in the oven. Old recipe, tried and true recipe, new recipe. Nada. They always turned out the same no matter how hard I tried.

Luckily, she'd already made them, and now all I had to do was take them out of the oven when they were done cooking.

Score one for me.

So as I busied myself with cooking the fried chicken and mashing potatoes, I thought about all that had happened today.

My beautiful house was no more. In its place was a shell of its former self.

But then I managed to smile as I remembered that Foster already had that part handled.

It'd be back to its old self in no time.

CHAPTER 14

I'm sorry for the things I said when you woke me up. Next time just bring me coffee and run. Fast.
-Sincerely, not a morning person

Blake

"Well that was the most awkward dinner of all time. Do you think your friends noticed anything wrong?" I asked Foster, falling forward onto his bed and slamming my face into a pillow.

Foster followed me into the bedroom, stopping at the bottom of the bed and said, "Nope."

His fingers started to work at my tennis shoes, unlacing them when I would've just kicked them off, and then placing them nicely on the floor.

My shorts were the next thing to go, and suddenly all of the sleep that'd been on my mind was gone in a flash. In its place was hot, sexy thoughts of the man currently pulling my panties over my ass.

He stopped once they were midway down my thighs, and kissed each ass cheek before biting lightly.

I jumped, pushing my hips into the bed as I looked at him over my shoulder.

"What," I said, turning over.

Then his eyes, which had been on my face, found my mound.

I blushed.

My face was on fire.

Luckily, I'd gotten into the habit of being totally shaved down there since I'd left David.

I don't know why. It'd just been something that he'd hated me doing, and now I kept it shaved out of spite.

Foster swallowed thickly, finally pulling his eyes away from my pussy to catch my eyes.

"I haven't had sex since my accident," he admitted, licking his lips nervously. "In fact, it was nearly four months before my accident. So it's been…a while."

I smiled, sitting up.

My hands found their way to his belt, hooking my fingers into the waistband of his jeans and pulling him closer to me.

"Take your shirt off," I ordered. "Now."

"Yes ma'am," he complied, ripping the shirt from his jeans where he'd tucked it in, and pulled it roughly over his head with a hand at the back of his collar.

He tossed it across the room, aiming for the dresser but not quite making it.

He did manage to knock over our drinks we'd gotten on the way home, though.

Neither one of us moved to clean it up. It didn't matter.

We'd deal with the mess. *Later.*

I worked the belt loose from his pants, dropping it on the bed beside my hips, before I started working on the button of his pants.

His eyes watched my movements, taking it all in with sharp, quick senses.

He allowed me to do what I wanted to do, and I was grateful.

I wanted this so bad I hurt.

I'd wanted Foster since the moment I saw him in the police headquarters' lobby.

I licked my lips once I worked the zipper down over his bulging erection, stopping before I went too far.

"Condoms," I said. "I think we need some."

He snorted, but turned and went into the bathroom, tossing me a look over his shoulder.

I licked my lips at seeing his pants hanging so low on his hips that I could see the top swells of his well-defined ass.

He came back moments later with a handful of condoms in his hand, tossing them down onto the bed beside his belt.

One knee planted in the bed at my feet, and he stopped, waiting for the next move.

I liked that he was deferring to me.

At least this time.

I suspected he wouldn't be so accommodating in the future.

My shaking and sweating hands went to the waistband of his black boxer briefs, and lowered it.

The first thing I saw was that he had a tattoo.

It made me freeze as I read the words.

"Does that…does that say what I think it says?" I asked, laughter gathering in my throat.

Looking up at him for confirmation, I couldn't help the laugh that burst free of my lips at the sheepish grin on his face.

"My brothers are dicks," he said. "I got drunk and then they proceeded to take me to the nearest tattoo shop where I got this."

I have a small wiener was tattooed in black bold letters just above the base of his cock.

And the saying couldn't be further from the truth.

Which I let him know the moment I saw his cock up close and personal.

It was massive.

Bigger than any I'd ever seen, which, granted, wasn't a lot, but he was also bigger than my purple eight inch dildo I'd bought after my divorce.

Easily.

"Oh, my," I said, placing my small hand onto his hard cock.

It was thick. So thick my hands could barely fit around it.

It was also soft. The skin felt like silk wrapped around a steel pole of muscle.

His cock was beautiful.

I'd never thought of cocks being much of anything before, but Foster's was just that.

Long, thick, with a darker mushroomed shaped head.

Veins popped out along his shaft, and one long, thick vein ran along the underside.

It even pulsed with the beat of his heart.

"Jesus," he hissed as my hands squeezed him tightly.

I smiled at him as I leaned forward, squeezing the head to milk out a pearl white droplet of pre-come.

He growled, and his fingers burrowed into my hair, not directing my movements. Rather, more so he could have something to hold onto.

I worked the tip of my tongue around the tip, circling the bulbous head with the front and back of my tongue before working my way down his shaft.

"I'm gonna come in your mouth," he said suddenly, yanking himself away from me.

I pouted at him.

"I hadn't even gotten a good taste," I teased.

He wrinkled his nose at me.

"That's okay," he murmured, stalking forward once again. "It's your turn now."

He stalked me.

As he moved forward, I moved backwards, putting more room in between us.

I did it with a smile on my face, though, which let him know that I was playing, and not scared.

"You're sure you want to play that way?" He asked carefully.

I blinked, and then lifted up onto my knees before turning my back to him.

Then, slowly, I lifted my shirt off my body, revealing my bare back to his gaze.

Then I slowly bent at the hips, waggling my butt at him.

"Well, big boy. You told me you had all the grand plans, yet I don't see you putting them into action," I teased.

Then he leaned forward, grasped my hips, and yanked me back until I was on the edge of the bed.

"This time," he rasped against the skin of my back. "I let you play your games. You've pretty much ruined my control, though."

Then I heard the foil of the condom ripping and looked over my shoulder in time to see him work the latex over his impressive cock.

I licked my lips before dropping down to let all my weight rest on my shoulders.

My hands were stretched out in front of me, grasping the pillow at the top of the bed.

His rough palm smoothed down my back, starting at the top of my spine, and running it down until it came to a rest just above the top of my ass.

And as if in a dream, he lifted his hand and slapped my ass.

I gasped, moving away from him slightly, but his hands were quick.

They grasped my waist and pulled me back into positon.

"Whoops," he teased.

I bit my lip to keep my moan of anticipation from bursting free.

Then he lined the head of his sheathed cock up with my entrance, and slowly started to sink the fat dick inside of me.

I felt full.

In fact, I'd felt full before he'd even gotten halfway in.

Then, by the time he got to three quarters of the way, I was already coming.

He froze, letting the pulsing spasm of my pussy clench and unclench around him for long moments before he started to sink slowly inside the rest of the way.

I was panting once he got his entire length inside of me. So full that I could barely draw a complete breath.

I swear I could feel him up by my navel.

But that had to be impossible...*right?*

He didn't give me much more time to think about it, though.

He made sure of it as he started to pull out all the way before he sank slowly back inside.

"You feel like heaven right now, and I'm not even bare inside of you. Jesus, this condom is the only thing keeping me from blowing my load way too early," he gritted out through clenched teeth.

I couldn't answer him. I was too busy focusing on me and how good I felt.

"Yes! God, yes Foster," I yelled, head thrown back in delight.

"*Yes, Foster. Yes!*" Boris echoed from the living room, causing us both to freeze.

Me with my head thrown back, and Foster with his cock half in, half out, of my pussy.

"Don't stop," I pleaded with him.

He slowly started forward again, pushing into me slowly at first before he picked the speed back up.

Soon my moans were back up to par, and Foster was back into his rhythm.

My eyes were closed, and I was too busy focusing on the way his fat cock head rubbed that spot inside of me that made me want to scream in ecstasy to think about anything else.

His hands took hold of my hips as he started to thrust faster. Harder.

His balls started to smack against me, hitting my clit with each thrust of his hips, causing that orgasm that I thought wasn't going to get there in time to start barreling towards me at a breakneck speed.

I licked my lips as I started to push back at him, reaching between my legs to press my clit with my fingers, working it in slow, circular motions.

Then his fingers started to rub my perineum, and I exploded.

Literally exploded.

I saw stars as my pussy clamped down hard on the intruder inside of me.

He groaned as he, too, started to come.

"Go, Foster! Harder Foster!" Boris sang.

His cock jerking inside of me as he worked me in slow, short thrusts.

My pussy was still pulsing as he rode me expertly with his cock, hitting just the right place that prolonged my orgasm into something more.

But just as suddenly as it came, it left me.

Panting and sweating.

"That bird…" Foster said from his collapsed state beside me.

His cock was pointed at the ceiling, and his spent release was gathered in the tip of the condom.

He didn't seem concerned, though.

So I didn't say anything either.

"The bird is weird," I said finally.

He snorted. "You can say that again."

"Boom goes the dynamite!" Boris sang.

Fucker.

CHAPTER 15

A real best friend makes your family question your sexuality.
-Fact of life

Foster

"At least you didn't lose your penis in the accident, too," Blake said helpfully.

I looked over at her and glared.

She giggled and sat up before she started to work my pants loose.

"It's easier if you take the blade off," I told her.

So she did.

She'd really been paying attention the other day at the fitting. She'd watched, learned, and comprehended everything that was said and done.

"How do you take a shower?" She asked. "With it on or off?"

I pointed to a pair of crutches in the corner. "Off. And I use the crutches."

She started removing my prosthesis, and before I knew it, I was laid bare before her.

"You know," she said, tracing the scar along my lower leg. "This isn't as small as I thought it'd be. Do you work it out as you would your other leg?"

I nodded. "Yeah. If you don't use it, you lose it, as my therapist says."

She nodded and stood up from the bed. "So...how about a sandwich? Then I want to throw a pot."

I blinked. "Why would you want to throw a pot? Is that something you normally do after making a sandwich?"

She grinned. "No. It's not even remotely close to what you're thinking."

Twenty minute later, I watched in rapture as Blake 'threw a pot' as I slipped my leg back into the prosthesis.

However, it wasn't 'throwing' an actual pot. It was making one.

"This is all in the hands." She demonstrated, putting her whole upper body into shaping the square of clay.

She dipped her hands into the water and came back to it, smoothing out more and more until she had the square of clay into an actual round...thing.

My eyes were glued to the wheel and the clay as it spun.

It was about the size of a large coffee can, and as I watched, she dipped her thumb into the top of it, burrowing out a hole.

"Alright," she said. "Pull up a chair and come sit down behind me. You can make it from here."

I did as she asked, placing the kitchen chair directly behind her stool and leaned forward.

"Dip your hands into the water and then place them directly on top of mine," she explained.

I did.

The clay was surprisingly cold under my hands.

It also felt incredibly weird, but at the same time extraordinarily cool.

"It's exactly like that scene in Ghost," I said laughingly.

She snorted. "Except we're a lot messier, and there's no way I'll have sex with you with all this mud all over me."

I leaned forward and bit her neck, causing her to jump and make the bowl go lopsided.

"Damn, that was looking pretty good, too," I frowned.

She did something with her fingers, pulling the pot slightly out, and fixed the wobble almost immediately. "There. Fixed."

I let my hands drop from hers as she got more in depth with the pot, amazed at how she made the pot so tall.

"I never would've thought you could make something like that with your hands," I said thoughtfully, letting my beard rasp against the soft skin of her shoulder.

She shivered.

"It takes practice," she said breathlessly. "Trust me, I didn't get this good overnight."

"No, I didn't think you did. You've got some real talent, though. I didn't see this stuff at your house at all. What did you do with the pottery that's finished?" I asked her, drawing a pattern in the mud covering her arm.

She snickered. "My parents' house. Well, their garage in particular. I have a whole shelf in there filled to the brim with my pottery. I moved it there after I broke up with David, and never moved it to my house."

"Tell me about him," I said softly.

She shrugged, body going tense.

"He ruined my life. Gave me hope and then took it all away," she whispered, taking her hands off the pot and standing up.

Which put her ass in my face.

Not that I was complaining.

She was wearing a t-shirt and panties.

Which meant there wasn't anything hindering my view because the t-shirt stopped just above her ass.

Her panties were cute, too.

Little pink bows decorated the sides, and lace lined the edges.

They were those cheekie ones that left half of the ass cheeks exposed, which inevitably drew my attention.

My hands met her ass, completely ignoring the fact that I was smearing clay all over her legs and butt cheeks.

"Hey!" She snapped. "Stop that."

I couldn't help myself.

I really couldn't.

"How much longer are you going to do that pot?" I asked, my dick suddenly impressively hard.

She snickered.

"Couple more minutes, you lusty boy," she tittered, bending over so that she could reach all the way inside of the pot. "Just don't move and startle me. This is the hard part."

I did what I was told, hands cupping both thighs as I waited for her to finish.

The whole time, though, I knew that we were about to get dirty.

I'd give her the couple minutes it took to get finished. But once that was done, I was fairly sure we'd be on the ground, going at it in the mud splashes.

And I was right.

***

I'd never slept in the same bed with a woman.

Not for a full night, anyway.

I was a get it done kind of guy.

I didn't waste time fucking around.

When I was with a woman, I got both of us off quickly, and then split just as fast.

With Blake, though, I found myself excited to do all those things I'd previously refused to do with other women.

I knew the minute my eyes opened that Blake was underneath me.

Partially, anyway.

My hand was cupping one breast, and my mouth was resting near the top of her head, sharing her pillow.

My other arm was stretched out underneath us both, and was just on the verge of unbearable.

My arm was asleep, and had been for some time if the state of feeling in my appendage was anything to go by.

Reluctantly, I rolled over, withdrawing my arm as carefully as I could. Although it turned out to be not so careful since I had no feeling in it.

I woke her.

She followed me as I rolled, spooning my back.

"I like being the big spoon," she said softly.

So softly that I wasn't really sure if she was awake or not.

"You're awake?" I asked her.

"Mm-hmm. For a couple minutes. I have to pee and I don't want to get up."

I just shook my head, burying my face into the pillows.

"You know where the bathroom is," I said, eyes closing at the exhaustion that pulled at me.

She left the bed with a little laugh, making very little noise.

So little, in fact, that I was nearly asleep again when she returned.

And stuck her cold as fuck feet right against my thigh.

"Fuck," I jolted, rolling over and pinning her to the bed. "You're dead."

Her eyes widened, and my arms moved until my hands were in the perfect spot, and I attacked.

"*Ahhhh*!" Blake screamed, giggling and squirming to get away from me.

I had her good, though.

I was straddling her waist, which kept her practically immobile as I tickled her ribs.

She laughed and thrashed, gasping in huge gulps of air as she screamed, "Stop!"

"What would you give me if I stopped?" I asked.

She glared through her giggles. "Anything."

"Anything?" I asked, turning the tickles into pinches as I zeroed in on her nipples.

She gasped, hips thrusting up as she said, "Please."

I grinned and eased off her hips.

Her shirt had ridden up to just underneath her breasts, and that's when I noticed that she wasn't wearing any panties.

"No panties, you naughty girl?" I asked.

She blushed. "I don't like wearing them. They get all up my ass when I sleep."

I snorted and bent down, taking in a deep breath, smelling the scent that came off her pussy.

"Smells like breakfast," I said, just before I bent down and licked the seam of her sex.

She shaved all the hair off down there, making the experience a lot different from my usual ones…when I had them that was.

Out of all the women I'd been with, Blake was the first one to shave herself completely.

And I found that I liked it.

A lot.

Groaning, she widened her legs as she said, "Breakfast of champions."

As she moved, the lips of her sex spread, revealing all the enticing little bits of herself that I just couldn't wait to bury myself inside.

I leaned down, letting the scruff of my beard run along the inside of her legs for a moment before I sucked her pretty little clit inside my mouth.

"Mmmm," I growled as her taste exploded in my mouth.

Sweet honey penetrated my taste buds as I ran my tongue in circles around her clit before moving down and plunging my tongue inside her entrance.

Her hands made a grab for my hair, but I caught both with mine before she could even touch it, forcing them to the bed as I moved up, pushing her legs high with my shoulders.

"Hold your legs," I demanded, letting go of her arms.

She did as she was told, like the good girl that she was, and pulled her legs back until they were touching her ribs.

My fingers, now free, moved until the ones from my left hand were spreading her open more completely at the top.

The others went down to her pussy and thrust up inside, two fingers thick.

My knuckles brushed her asshole, causing that enticing pucker to clench in response.

When she didn't move away, I did it again, causing her to moan and move down to allow my fingers to move deeper inside of her.

Knowing I'd explore that option later, I withdrew my fingers and mouth, and crawled up her body.

My cock came to a rest against her overheated pussy lips and I started to thrust, running my cock up the seam of her lips as I bent down and took her mouth.

She moaned and wrapped her arms around my shoulders, moving with me as I did.

Each time my cock hit her clit, she would jump, causing her distended nipples to scrape deliciously over my chest.

Lifting up, I grabbed her knees and pushed them together, creating an improvised sheath with the lips of her sex and her thighs.

My movements became faster as the pressure became extreme.

Her pussy was practically gushing, covering me in her juices as I thrust.

Her eyes were glazed as she watched me move.

Reaching down, I pushed her shirt up over her breasts and pinched her nipples, causing her to jump and cant her hips.

Which, in turn, caused my cock to enter something completely different than the tunnel I'd created with her legs and pussy lips.

And let me tell you something, this was fifty thousand times better.

The walls of her vagina surrounded my cock like it was made to fit me.

I'd never, in my entire life, been inside someone completely bare.

And right now, with Blake, it felt just…*right*.

Her eyes were stunned as I started to move inside of her, just as surprised as I was that I was now inside of her.

"You feel fucking perfect," I grunted, moving faster.

My balls started to slap against her ass, and I finally lost control.

All of my senses were on overload as I started to pound into her.

"Oh, God," she said, lifting her hands to play with her nipples, plucking and pinching. "Harder."

Taking a hold of her legs at the backs of her knees, I pushed until I had perfect control of her pussy. Giving her exactly what she wanted.

The new angle must've allowed me to hit something inside of her that really worked for her, because it wasn't ten seconds later that she started to come.

"Fuck!" She screamed, back arching as best as she could manage.

"*Oh, God yes, Foster!*" Boris screeched.

I ignored him.

Mostly because her walls started to pulse, causing my eyes to cross in pleasure.

Ripping myself from her juicy core abruptly, I started to come the moment my dick met the cool air.

Hot cum spurted from the tip of my cock, jetting all the way up to her bare breasts, then again up to her belly button before I could control my cock enough to push it down onto her bare pussy.

"Goddammit," I groaned, grunting out the rest of my release. "You've got a voodoo pussy that makes me do stupid things."

She laughed, taking one finger and trailing it in the release I'd adorned her stomach with, before bringing it up to her mouth and sucking it clean.

"Fuck me."

She winked at my statement. "I already did."

CHAPTER 16

A relationship is made for two. It's just that some hoe's don't know how to count.
-Fact of Life

Foster

"You wanna go get something to eat?" She asked me forty five minutes later as she slipped on her shirt.

I squinted over at the clock, tired beyond belief.

Not from the sex, but just tired in general.

But I felt better than I had in months.

Groaning, I pushed myself out of bed and sat on the edge.

The first thing I did was rub some lotion into the skin surrounding my scar.

I had to make sure I did that, or the skin would degrade. Or so I'd been told.

I'd yet to experience a blister, but I was fairly sure it'd happen sooner or later.

"Here," Blake said, handing me the sleeve that held the pin onto my leg.

"Thanks," I said, slipping it on carefully to discourage any air bubbles. "Where do you want to go eat?"

As I continued the process of getting dressed, I watched her carefully.

She was wearing red and white tights, a blue jean skirt, and a bright blue shirt that said, *One Fish, Two Fish, Red Fish, Blue Fish* on it.

Then she started to braid her hair.

"What are you wearing?" I asked.

There was a smile in my voice that I couldn't hide, and she tossed a grin over her shoulder at me.

"It's officially Dr. Seuss day," she told me.

"You're allowed to wear that to work?" I clarified.

She nodded. "It wasn't my idea to dress like this. But I'll do it. I have no problem looking dorky. It's only if you have a problem with going out to eat with me in this."

I shrugged and pulled the pants on that I'd set out the night before.

Then pulled on my shoes.

"Do you think if you asked them if you could buy only one shoe, they'd allow you to?" She questioned, causing me to look up.

"I highly doubt it, to be honest."

"Well maybe ask them if you can have it for half price…since, you know, you're not going to use the other shoe," she offered.

I winked. "I think I can handle paying for two shoes."

She shrugged. "I'll bet they give a military discount."

I gave her a pointed look. "I can handle it. And how'd we get to talking about shoes, anyway? How much longer do we have before I need to take you to work?"

She spun around, surprise evident on her face. "Why would I need you to take me to work?"

I shook my head. "You had somebody break into your house, and a drive by shooting aimed at your house. I'm sorry, but you'll just have to deal with me taking you to work unless you want me to start getting forceful."

She held up her hands in mock horror.

"Ooooo!" She sang sarcastically.

I vaulted out of bed, catching her around the hips before she could even make it to the bedroom doorway.

"Eeek!" She squealed as I picked her up and tossed her over my shoulder.

She laughed breathlessly.

"Put me down, you big oaf!"

"Yes, ma'am!"

Then I threw her across the room, relishing in the scream that came out of her mouth before she hit the bed.

"You're so dead," she declared a few minutes later after I got out of the bathroom.

"You haven't moved yet," I said, walking over to the closet and pulling my Kevlar vest out.

I turned and watched her watch me as I put my vest on, her eyes studied my movements as I fit the vest to where it'd sit most comfortably.

"My daddy's is black," she said.

I nodded. "My department issued one is, too. But I've taken a liking to this one."

"Why? It looks kind of ratty, to be honest," she said, sitting up onto her elbows, letting her feet hang off the bed as she did so.

I pointed to the signature in the bottom right corner of my vest.

"I got this one about three years ago. It was my last year as a SEAL," I explained. "That's my brother's signature. I did the same for him. It was stupid," I shrugged. "But I'm a superstitious man. I use what I know will work."

"You don't trust the ones you got from the police department?" She asked, standing up all the way.

She really did look ridiculous, but she looked pretty hot, too.

"Yes, I do. It's just not mine." I hesitated before sitting down on the bed. "Are you sure you're allowed to wear that to work?"

She grinned. "I guess we'll see."

***

Blake

I slipped out of the truck, landing on my feet with a slight thunk.

My feet crunched in the gravel as I turned to close the door.

Foster was just rounding the truck when the first person saw what I was wearing.

"I shouldn't have worn this," I muttered to myself.

"What'd you say?" Foster asked as he met me on my side of his truck.

I didn't say anything as I turned to face the man walking towards us.

If you could call him a man at all.

"Hey," David said. "I'm glad to see that you're okay."

I shrugged and turned to walk into the building, more than ready to get away from the stupid man in front of me.

The one at my back, though, was a different story.

I could stay in his arms all day long.

He also did really well at keeping me from wanting to punch David in the nose. Mostly by distracting me, and distract me he did once we reached the top of the steps.

I hadn't realized that he'd followed me as close as he had, because the moment my hand touched the door handle, it was suddenly gone.

Then, as if in a real life Disney movie, he swept me up into his arms and kissed me silly.

I whore moaned, leaning into him and threading my arms around his neck.

My fingers buried in what little hair he had, and the feel of his gun digging into my hip did nothing to my raging libido that was on hyper drive after last night

"Have a good shift," he said breathlessly. "I'll see you when you get off. Don't go out for lunch."

With that, he dropped me to my feet, walked to the door, and ushered me inside.

Dazedly, I walked inside, not surprised in the least to find the entire station *oohing* and *ahhing* over our display.

"That a boy, Crush!" Someone yelled from the back of the station.

Foster didn't acknowledge anyone, as was his way.

I, on the other hand, said hi to at least fifteen people before I finally made it back to dispatch offices.

"That was some show!" Pauline crowed the moment I walked inside.

I shook my head.

"How'd you even see it?" I asked.

"Get to work, ladies," an annoyed man's voice said from the doorway.

I resisted the urge to bug my eyes out at Pauline as I dropped into my chair and put on my headset.

"Alright, ladies! Let's make this a good one!" Our boss, Bradley, said.

I hadn't made my mind up yet when it came to Bradley.

He was a smart man, and a police officer.

Or had been before he'd gotten hurt.

Now he had to have a permanent desk job because his leg wouldn't allow him to do the normal daily living activities most women and men did daily without realizing it.

He was pushy, and thought he was better than everyone else.

He was the same thing that we were. Dispatchers.

My phone rang and I forgot all about Bradley.

I wouldn't think about him until much later.

At the end of my shift, to be exact.

***

"Unit 4 responding to a 10-46," Foster's voice came in over the radio.

I shivered.

Jesus, the man was sexy.

Even his voice sounded sexy.

It was going on our seven and a half of my eight hour shift, and I was so ready to be at Foster's place it wasn't even funny. The lack of sleep last night was really getting to me. I would kill for a nap right now.

I was also looking forward to doing other things, too.

Thirty more minutes. Thirty more minutes.

I kept chanting the words to myself, praying that I could stay awake.

It'd been dead all night, and this was the first time I'd actually heard Foster's voice over the radio the entire time.

"10-4, unit 4," I said, keeping the line open as I waited for him to help the stranded motorist.

10-46, I'd learned, was when a motorist was stranded in a broken down car. That, or the car was abandoned all together.

Long minutes passed as I checked out my nails, wondering if I should get a pedicure before this weekend.

I'd agreed to go with Foster to attend a party that his brother was throwing for their little girl's third birthday.

I was fairly sure they wouldn't care what my nails looked like, but…

A garbled, muffled sound abruptly echoed through my headset, and I looked up, staring blankly at my monitor.

I wasn't really sure what I was hearing.

It almost sounded like a…

Bang. Bang. Bang.

Gunshots didn't sound like I'd thought they'd sound, but they were unique nonetheless.

"Unit 4, 10-101?" I fairly screamed.

I could see Pauline stand in my peripheral vision, but she stayed there, waiting for my go.

More scuffling sounded and I heard the labored breathing of someone before Foster's strained voice said, "Need help."

"Pauline, he needs backup," I said urgently, before my fingers started to flow over the keyboards, putting in information, dispatching units, and alerting those who needed to know.

My heart, however, was freakin' pounding.

My stomach was roiling, and I felt wetness hitting my cheeks, letting me know that I was crying.

I didn't let that stop me from doing my job, though.

Scuffling continued to sound, and then one more shot rang out.

Then nothing.

Absolutely nothing.

I was so scared that Foster was dead, that when his voice came back on the radio, I visibly wilted in my seat.

"Unit 4, 10-106," Foster growled breathlessly. "I'll need an ambulance for the man that just tried to shoot me in the face."

I dispatched the ambulance, alerted other officers, and then promptly threw up.

I dashed for the trashcan across the room, barely making it in time before I lost my lunch.

Jesus Christ on a cracker, the man had scared the absolute shit out of me.

I made it back to my seat, eyes glazed, and collapsed into it.

My head hit the desk, and I started to cry silently.

"Take a break, Rhodes," Bradley ordered. "And good job."

I ignored him, going back to my Solitaire game I'd been playing before the call had come in, but I wasn't into it.

I lost.

Badly.

My mind was a jumbling roil of emotions as I waited for the clock to strike eight.

Once I'd heard that Foster had made it back to the station, I gave Pauline a wave and vaulted out of my chair, forgetting completely that I was connected to the headset.

It yanked off my head once I'd reached the limit on its length, and slammed against the desk in my wake.

I didn't stop, though.

Instead, I kept going, running through the doors to the bull pen, and straight through the lobby outside.

I saw him there, talking to his brother, and I didn't stop to think.

I just launched myself into his arms, holding him to me tightly.

He took a step back, the SUV at his back stopping him from going any further, and gathered me to him.

After I kissed him, I started to berate him.

"You scared the absolute shit out of me!" I yelled loudly into his face.

He grinned weakly. "Yeah, I see that. It seems to be a trend tonight," he said as he looked over my shoulder at his brother.

His hands were resting on my ass, holding me up, so I twisted and looked at Miller.

He was looking at his brother with relief, love, and a little bit of annoyance.

He kissed my forehead, and then let me slip down to my feet before he said, "Do you mind hanging with Miller here while I go talk to the chief?"

I looked at him suspiciously, but nonetheless nodded and said, "Sure."

"I'll be done quickly. Just need to give him a report of what happened, and then go from there, okay?" He confirmed.

I nodded again, and he disappeared into the building.

"So…" I said, looking at his brother once the door shut behind Foster. "What do you think really happened?"

He winked at me. "That's the twenty three thousand dollar question."

***

Foster

"He was waiting for me," I said to the chief. "I know it like I know my last name's Spurlock."

The chief sighed and leaned back into his seat, rubbing his eyes with his hands. "Tell me why you think that. From what I gathered from the cops that questioned him, you startled him…or so he says."

I shook my head.

"I passed that same freakin' street ten times tonight. You told me to watch for the party that we suspected would be taking place, and so I kept running different routes, practically making a figure eight," I said. "I saw that man on the first street and didn't think anything of it. Then he moved to the next street I was on. After the fifth time I saw him, I finally pulled up."

He nodded, motioning with his hand for me to continue.

"I didn't actually see him until I walked up to the car. He was lying in the backseat, fully dressed. When I asked him to step out, he did. Peacefully. Then when I started to walk back to the cruiser with his license and registration, he moved. If I hadn't turned back around to ask him a question about his license, he would've shot me in the back of the head."

"Jesus, what a clusterfuck," Chief Rhodes said tiredly.

I nodded. "A Charlie Foxtrot indeed."

"Well you'll be glad to know that the mobile fingerprinting unit got a match on him. For quite a few offenses, in fact. Only one of which being the print we pulled from Mercy's house and the break-in a few weeks ago," the Chief said.

My teeth gritted, and suddenly I didn't feel so bad about shooting him in the belly three times with his own gun.

"Has he said anything?" I asked forcefully.

The chief shook his head once. "Nada. I have Greer on it, though. If there's anything to find, Greer will let me know."

I rubbed my chest, feeling a bruise already forming from where the bullet had slammed into my Kevlar vest.

"What's that on your…foot?" The Chief asked when he stood.

I looked down at my foot and grimaced.

"I think it's skin," I said. "He fell on it."

The Chief's expression soured. "That's just…disgusting."

He handed me a disinfectant wipe out of the tub he kept at the corner of his desk.

"Get that cleaned up. I can tell you from experience that Blake pukes at the sight of blood," he said.

I bent down and scrubbed the blood and bits of…stuff, off my prosthesis. Then threw the towel in the trash next to The Chief's desk.

Wiping my hands with some hand sanitizer, I stood and looked at him.

"This all has to do with her, doesn't it?" I asked point blank.

He shrugged. "Best guess, yes. I just don't know what she's done to warrant it. That doesn't mean that I won't be finding out, though."

I nodded.

"Well, she won't be leaving my sight, that's for sure."

As I exited the chief's office I heard him say, "I never doubted you would. Just make sure you state your intentions to Shank before you get too involved with her."

That was something I really, really didn't want to do.

Not that I didn't plan on having Blake as my own, because I did. But because I didn't want to talk to that man period until I had this situation ironed out.

Would I talk to him anyway? *Yes.*

Would I enjoy it? *Fuck no.*

CHAPTER 17

Who lit the fuse on your tampon?
-T-shirt

Foster

I opened the door to my apartment, not surprised in the least to see Blake's father standing on my doorstep.

Blake had fallen asleep on the couch during the movie I'd insisted we watch, and had been sleeping for over an hour.

Not wanting to wake her, because I knew exactly where this conversation was going, I grabbed my gun from the coffee table, shoved it in the back of my pants, and met him in the hallway.

He watched my movements with the eyes of a trained officer.

Someone that had been there and done that so many times that they could anticipate the movements of another officer before it was even done.

His eyes, though, stalled on the body of his daughter as she laid on the couch, and his eyes snapped to mine, all of a sudden furious.

I hurried outside before he could start demanding answers, closing it behind me before I leaned against the wall and waited for it.

"Why's she been crying?" Lou demanded.

I sighed.

Then started telling him about my night, followed by what the chief had told me before I'd left.

"Fuck me," he said, turning around to pace back and forth in the hallway. "I haven't found shit. I've pulled every goddamned marker I had, and still have nothing to show for it. I'm going to have to dig deeper."

I didn't doubt that the man had markers. I also expected that he had a lot of the criminal underground in his back pockets.

You didn't stay a cop for as long as he had and not know a few criminals that you could call on if you needed them.

"I have a couple of computer savants working on it through a buddy of mine. I also have my brother's club president working on it from his end," I said.

"Silas Mackenzie?" He asked, surprised.

I nodded, not surprised that he knew the men associated with my brother. I was fairly positive he had a file twelve inches thick on me and my family.

"How'd...never mind. I'm sure I don't want to know," I said, shaking my head. "He was...is CIA, I think. I haven't really been able to figure out exactly what he is. I'm not sure he ever got out. Anyway, I digress. He's pulling anything he knows about Bryson Bullard, the man that tried to shoot me tonight."

The Shank came out to play, then.

He pulled out his phone and dialed a number, not looking at me as he started talking low into the phone.

I couldn't make out much of his conversation, but what I did hear, I knew was definitely on the opposite side of the line that one tried not to cross as an officer of the law.

"I don't care what you have to do, you stupid son of a bitch. Either you get him to talk, or I will, and you really, *really* won't like it," he hissed before he hung up.

My brows raised as he turned around and stared blankly at me.

"What'd you just do?" I asked curiously.

He smiled.

"A daddy has a duty to his daughter. If she's hurt, I'm hurt. I'm not going to fucking fail in this. It'll be over my dead body that she'll have to endure another day like two days ago. She'd be dead and gone right now if it wasn't for your friends," he growled. "Now, you do your job protecting my girl, and I'll do mine."

With that cryptic comment, he turned and started down the hall.

His wide, strong shoulders bunched with tension as he went.

"Lou?" I called to his retreating back.

He froze, and turned around slowly.

"No," he said. "You haven't known her long enough yet."

I grinned. "You realize that's not going to stop me, right? That I do plan on doing it whether I have your permission or not. I just wanted you to know my intentions. I'd planned on waiting until all of this was over, but I changed my mind."

***

I lifted Blake into my arms, carrying her effortlessly into the bedroom.

She didn't even stir as I laid her on the bed, and threw the covers over her.

She made the cutest little groan as she settled deeper into the bed, and it took all I had not to roll her over and start fucking her before she was even awake.

Alas, I turned on my heel and ran through my nightly routine of trimming my beard, washing my hands and face, and slicking on some deodorant and removing my prosthesis before getting into bed.

I slipped under the covers and slid into the middle, all too aware of my missing limb as I pulled Blake into my arms.

She curled her legs around my leg, and snuggled deeply into my chest before giving another cute sigh, and falling back to sleep.

I was nearly asleep myself when the pager on my nightstand went off, alerting me to a SWAT call.

"Motherfucker," I breathed.

CHAPTER 18

When the scent on his pillow has to be enough.
-Night shift wife

Foster

"You're the bomb," I said to Alice as I let her into the living room.

Alice was a fellow police officer that lived downstairs.

I was lucky as fuck that she was at home, otherwise I would've been torn on leaving Blake by herself. Especially with the shit storm that was swirling above her head lately.

"You're welcome, Foster. I just wish you'd have called me for something other than to babysit your woman," her sultry voice said from behind me.

I winced.

Yeah, we'd slept together before.

It'd been convenient, but neither one of us had been looking for anything but a good time.

Something that we got, and then left soon afterwards.

"Whatever you do, don't piss her off. Her uncle is the Chief. Trust me, you don't want any of her kind of trouble," I ordered, tossing her a look over my shoulder.

She tossed me a glare that clearly showed how scared she really was.

"And whatever you do, don't tell her we've slept together. I want her to stay where she's at, which totally defeats the entire purpose of having you here if you piss her off and make her leave," I explained, picking up my keys from the table.

"Whatever," Alice said.

I winced.

Alice, although a cop, was also a girl.

She had hormones, and mood swings just like the rest of the female population.

She was also pissy that I hadn't called her in a while.

She was a professional, though, and enjoyed her job.

I also saw her as a friend I could count on, which was why I was trusting her with one of the most important things in my world.

Something that kind of startled me. Especially since it'd been so short of a time period since we'd met.

"Thank you, Alice," I said. "Make yourself at home."

I stopped though, turning back around. "Except my room. Don't go in there unless you have to."

She flipped me off, and I left with a smile on my face.

When I got to the station, though, I wasn't smiling at all.

"What do you mean you're afraid of heights?" Luke said, yelling. "You were a fuckin' SEAL!"

"Hey man, back the fuck off," I said as we got into Rita.

Rita was actually an armored truck. Something that was made to withstand a shit ton of violence and keep on truckin'.

I wasn't really sure who'd started calling the truck Rita, but it was permanent now, and didn't look to be changing ever again.

"I said I was nervous around heights. I never said anything about being scared of them. I'll still do my job," I snarled. "And what's your fuckin' problem tonight?"

Luke grimaced. "Reese started picking up shifts on the cardiology floor at the hospital. That's one floor away from the fuckin' roof where we're going. I don't like her there, but she's stuck."

That explained that.

Immensely.

I'd be short, too, had I been in his shoes.

Luckily, though, the man we were going to the hospital to get out was on the roof.

Which meant that the man wouldn't be able to get back off the roof without a badge to scan him back in.

The trip there was spent talking schematics of the hospital, what we were going to do, and if we were to take lethal force if needed.

As I entered the hospital behind Luke, I stopped abruptly when a familiar pair of shoulders, and a steely pair of eyes caught mine before he disappeared around the corner.

"What the fuck?" I asked, startled.

Why was Lou here?

And if he was here, why was he leaving when there was clearly a hostage situation going on upstairs?

He couldn't lie to me and tell me he didn't know.

That man knew shit before other people even had time to report it.

Yet I didn't have the time to dwell on the fact because we heard the man that had tried to kill me earlier start screaming.

We couldn't tell what he was saying, though. It all just sounded like a bunch of gibberish from this far down.

He was really yelling, too.

I followed Luke, not sparing Lou another thought as we made it through security and straight to the stairs.

The elevator had been temporarily turned off, the only people that could override it were us, medical personnel that would need it in case of an emergency, and the fire department.

No one would be coming in or out without us knowing.

"Alright, boys," Luke said as we climbed the last flight of stairs. "Stay safe and stay sharp."

Something that Luke said every single time we entered a situation such as the one we were about to head into.

Nico slammed the door open with a booted foot, and immediately passed through the open door, dropping down to his knees to allow Michael, who'd been behind him, a clear shot.

It was for naught, though.

Bryson Bullard didn't even turn to look at us as we came out.

"You can't do this, old man! I'm fuckin' protected!" Bullard screamed.

Instead, his eyes were focused on the building across the street, at a certain window, in particular.

"James, what's he lookin' at?" I asked.

James was the sniper for the SWAT team, and a man damn good at his job.

However, what Bullard was looking at was not James, seeing as James was in a building catty corner to the one that Bullard was currently shouting at.

"You won't take me alive!" Bryson Bullard screamed, turning to us. "That crazy fucking guy can…"

He suddenly focused somewhere behind us, and started screaming. "I'm so dead. I'm sorry!"

"Do you think he's using?" Nico asked me.

I shrugged, aiming my gun at the man.

He had a huge fucking Oxygen tank strapped to his chest. Duct tape was wrapped around his middle, holding the tank in place, and he was scanning the surroundings of the roof like a man possessed.

"I won't tell you!" He screamed, spittle spraying a three foot radius in front of him.

None of us moved, all of us backed up against the side of the building while the man screamed at the edge of the hospital's roof.

I knew that if we weren't careful with where we placed our bullets, the man would fucking blow up if they tore through the tank.

"If we don't do something, he's going to jump over, and then where will we be?" Bennett, who was on the other side of me, rumbled.

We didn't get a chance to answer.

"You're daughter's a hot fucking piece, and I'm sorry I'll never get the chance to fuck her properly! Just remember that I'll be taking the name of the man who plans to take her with me to the grave! You'll never get…" Bullard screamed as he raised a gun.

Although it wasn't pointed at us, we all tensed.

BOOM!

The rooftop exploded.

Or at least felt like it had.

What was more probable was that the man in front of us had exploded.

Bits and pieces of...*ick*...flesh, blood, and matter, exploded around us as Bullard's body was blown to smithereens.

"What...the...fuck," Michael breathed. "I've never seen anything like that. And I was a fuckin' marine for years."

I snorted.

Nobody really knew what Michael had done before he'd come to Kilgore.

We knew he had a mother and a father, and that he was in the Marines.

What we didn't know why he was the way he was. Why he didn't date. And why he disappeared every five days...somewhere.

What I did know about him, was that he had my back no matter what.

He would forever protect the entire team with his life, and little impressed him.

Right now, though, he was beyond impressed.

As was I.

Along with every man on the team.

"What happened?" Downy yelled frantically through the headset.

Downy was our negotiator. He'd been on the bullhorn down below with the Chief.

Which meant he'd missed the show.

"I think it's in my hair," Bennett whispered, thoroughly disgusted.

I didn't even want to think about things being in my hair. For now I'd just ignore it.

It wasn't the first time, and it certainly wouldn't be the last.

"Who shot?" Luke yelled.

Luke was pissed.

Which I guess he had a right to be.

However, as far as I knew, none of us had shot.

"Negative."

"Not me."

"Nope."

"Nada."

"Wasn't me."

The last one had been James. His confusion was just as apparent in his tone as it was in ours.

Luke growled in frustration as he walked further out on the roof.

"Well, it had to be one of you!" He snarled.

I started ejecting the shells from my shotgun, as did the others.

"All accounted for, boss," I said, handing him my shells.

His eyes narrowed at me, but then widened.

"Well, if it wasn't y'all…who the fuck was it?" He finally asked.

Again with the thirty nine thousand dollar questions.

There was only one possibility, though.

If it wasn't us, then it had to be someone else.

And that someone else never touched us.

There'd only been one shot, and that had been aimed at Bullard.

***

Blake

I woke up and stretched my arms up high over my head, rolling over as I did.

I felt freakin' wonderful.

I'd gotten more than enough sleep last night, sleep that had been denied to me over the past few weeks.

And I could thank Foster for that.

When he'd suggested we watch a movie, I'd been wary.

I wasn't a big fan of horror, but it turned out that that didn't even matter.

I was asleep within the first thirty minutes, totally forgoing all the scary parts.

The first thing that I became aware of as the sleep cleared from my brain was that Foster was gone, and had been for some time.

His side of the bed was cold.

Which made me wonder…why?

He'd been just as tired as I'd been last night, and he'd promised that he'd wake me when he went on his morning run.

What I could tell, though, by the sun streaming through the windows was that it wasn't even morning anymore.

It was going into the afternoon.

Standing up, I walked into the bathroom to take care of my morning ritual before heading to the living room to look for Foster.

Who I found instead was anyone *but* Foster.

There was a woman in Foster's living room.

A beautiful woman.

"Who are you?" I snapped at the cute blonde on Foster's couch.

The woman looked up and smiled.

Although it came out more pained than anything.

Her eyes took in my pantless state, as well as Foster's shirt, before she dismissed me.

"Alice. I'm Foster's neighbor; I also work with him on the force. Foster got called out in the middle of the night for a SWAT situation," she explained. "He didn't want to wake you."

I gritted my teeth at the slight curl of disgust her words carried when she'd said the last part.

"How long has he been gone?" I asked.

"Six hours," she clipped.

I decided that maybe I wouldn't bother talking to her anymore.

Turning on my heel, I walked back to the bedroom and slipped on a pair of black shorts.

A pair which happened to be Foster's.

I was happy with them, though, since I planned on throwing a pot or two while I waited.

I was fairly sure he wouldn't care, either.

After taking care of that little tidbit, I walked back out to the living room and started to gather my things.

Since what I planned to do today was a large vase, I cut a much bigger piece of clay with my wire instead of the small one I'd used with Foster the previous time.

We both stayed silent as I started to get the things collected that I'd need.

I was fully aware of her assessing me, even though she never bothered looking up from her magazine.

As I sat down, she finally deigned to speak to me again.

"So, you're a *dispatcher*?" She asked offhandedly.

I looked up at her sharply, not liking the tone she used to say dispatcher.

She might as well had called me a garbage man.

"Sure am," I said.

"How come I've never seen you?" Alice asked, not bothering to look up from her magazine.

It was one of Foster's Guns and Ammo ones that he had on his nightstand.

I remembered it distinctly because it had a pink gun on the front, and there'd been a little blurb that was asking if it was okay to make guns look '*pretty*.'

I'd actually wanted to read that article, but I'd left it on the nightstand to get to when I got a chance.

And I knew Foster had already read the entire thing since we'd had our own debate on whether guns should be made to look like that.

His main argument had been about kids.

How they'd, if the gun was left within reach, be more tempted by a gun that was pretty rather than a gun that was just plain black.

In fact, I'd argued with him about it, and had meant to read the article, but he'd put his foot down that we'd be watching a movie, so I'd left it in the bedroom.

Which meant that she had to come in the bedroom.

And she'd seen me naked.

What the fuck?

Rather than dwelling on it, I got some water on my hands, and pressed the pedal with my foot to get the wheel spinning.

Then I started to press my fingers into the clay, moving them up to form the base of the vase.

"So what do you think of him?" Alice said sometime later.

I'd just started to work the vase up about nine inches in height when she'd said the words, and accidentally pressed harder than I'd meant to, making it lean slightly to one side.

Sighing, I fixed it before I stood and started to press inward. "What do I think about whom?"

"Foster," she answered quickly, finally looking up at me.

Something which I caught out of the corner of my eye.

I didn't look at her, though, so totally focused on my vase that I didn't even care enough to look up.

"I love him," I said simply.

It was true. I loved him.

Something which didn't scare the shit out of me like I'd thought it would.

When I'd left David, I'd had a party to celebrate our split.

A party of one where I got drunk, and then passed out in my rented hotel room.

But it'd been fun.

However, I'd made a promise to myself that night that I'd never let myself fall apart over a guy.

A promise that I broke the first day I met Foster Lager Spurlock.

A promise that I was happy to break.

I knew in my heart that Foster was a good man.

When he'd expressed his disgust over David's behavior, I'd felt relief.

Utter relief that there were still good men in this world that weren't taken.

"You love him?" She asked slowly. "You've only known him for like a month."

I ignored her, thinking it'd be best to not bring attention to the fact that she was getting to me.

"He's not a love kind of guy. He's a fuck and go home kind of guy," she said, turning to face me now.

She was wearing short shorts that rode up to her vagina, and a skin tight tank top that had some sort of police symbol on it.

How did the woman become a police officer?

She was the epitome of dainty, dumb blonde. Which was saying something since I was blonde myself.

How'd a woman like her become a cop?

I'd heard that the KPD's fitness test was one of the hardest in the State of Texas to pass.

Did she have to suck someone's cock to get them to pass her?

"You know, when he called my number last night, I was fairly sure he was calling me to come up to his apartment for a completely different reason," she said snidely.

The insinuation in that comment had me backing away from the table before I could even think better of myself.

Once my foot left the wheel, the spinning vase slowed slowly, before stopping completely.

Once I was sure it would stay where I wanted it, I walked purposefully to the woman, muddy hands and all, and stopped until I was toe to toe with her.

She'd stood once she saw me coming towards her, quickly dropping the magazine on the table and squaring her shoulders.

"So tell me," I said, eyeing her. "What's your malfunction?"

She moved forward, putting her face into mine before poking me in the chest.

"He's mine," she hissed. "I've been waiting for him to come back. I had to give him time because of his handicap. He was so good, he's worth the wait."

I scrunched my eyebrows at her. "He's not handicapped. And if he wanted to be with you, he'd have been with you. His dick wasn't affected, it was his leg. And Foster doesn't do things half assed. If he wanted you again, he'd have had you. Which means only one thing. He doesn't want you."

I heard the lock on the door click open, and heard the *tink-step* of Foster walking into the room.

Did I turn around and face him?

No.

I stayed looking at Alice, who also kept her eyes on me.

"I'll just let you know now that I won't give up," she hissed quietly before she backed up, picked up her phone and keys from the coffee table, and walked around the table as if she hadn't a care in the world.

When I turned around, I was stunned to see that Foster was going out into the hall with her instead of coming to me.

Just…what?

As I watched the door close behind him, I turned on my heel and went back to my wheel, wetting my hands once again, and finishing my vase.

Other than a few problems, like the fingernail mark at the very top, and the thicker lip on one side of the opening, it was pretty good.

All things considering.

Although once I had it finished, and removed from the wheel, I wasn't up to throwing anymore pots.

Not the kind I usually threw, anyway.

After ten minutes of still no Foster, I went to the sink, washed my hands, and then got into the shower.

I made sure to lock the door, though, just in case he tried to come in.

He didn't.

When I got out, I dried quickly off and walked into his bedroom.

Kind of surprised to see him sitting on the edge of the bed, watching the bathroom door.

He looked at me.

"What's wrong?" He asked.

I glanced up at him as I walked to my bag in the corner.

Slipping the panties on underneath the towel, I said, "Wrong? Whatever would give you that idea?"

My sarcasm knob was on full blast.

And he could tell.

His eyebrows rose. "What's that supposed to mean? Alice said there was nothing wrong."

I snorted. "That's rich."

Slipping my bra on, I followed it up with a short pair of shorts that were beyond indecent, and a tank top that said, '*I love country boys*.'

Before I could pull the shirt all the way down, though, Foster was there.

"Tell me," he growled, eyes hot with ire.

"I don't want to talk to some chick about how good you are in bed. This isn't a Kum-by-fucking-ya. I'm a real blood and bone woman. I don't like sharing, and I've already proved that fact by divorcing my ex-husband who, apparently, had no problem with sharing. Maybe you ought to think about that next time before you call some old flame to watch over me," I hissed at Foster. "One, who might I had, still wants to fuck you."

I surprised myself with the amount of venom I was able to pour into that little speech. Which apparently surprised Foster, too.

"She said…what?" He asked incredulously, not moving back at all.

"You fucking heard me."

He blinked, pushing into me until my back was pressed against the wall.

"I know you're pissed, but I don't know what your deal is. What she said is not on me. What she said is on her," he snapped. "Maybe you should stop thinking that every man is like that piece of shit you married."

I glared at him.

"Get off me," I hissed.

He stepped back, giving me the space I'd asked for.

Irrationally disappointed that he'd stepped back from me, giving me the space I'd requested, I walked past him into the bathroom.

"Just leave me alone," I said as I slammed the bathroom door.

"Do you still want to come to the party with me?" Foster growled through the door.

Opening the door, I glared at him, letting him know just what I wanted to do with his severed head with my eyes alone, and nodded once.

"Yeah, I want to go to your fucking party with you," I snarled.

Then I slammed the door again.

Or tried to.

He caught it before the door could latch, forcing it open.

Which, in turn, forced me backwards.

I was still mad.

He was still mad that I was mad at him.

Which meant, when his mouth slammed down on mine, our kiss was angry.

It wasn't a soft kiss, either.

It was hot, hard, and heavy.

He nipped my lip hard, pulling back only long enough to take a hold of my shorts, rip the button free of the hole, and yank them forcefully down my legs.

I heard a tearing sound, surprised when I felt a rush of excitement between my legs with the force he was using.

Without any foreplay whatsoever, he twirled me around, and pushed me down roughly over the bathroom counter.

My shirt and bra were immediately soaked by the water that'd been leftover from my morning routine, making my white tank top transparent.

My nipples hardened as I looked up, watching him rip his own zipper down, eyes zeroed in on mine in the mirror.

He didn't waste time ripping a condom out of his wallet and slicking it on over his length.

By the time the end of the condom covered all that it could cover, I was practically panting in need.

Neither one of us said a word as he line his massive cock up with my pussy and slammed inside.

He filled me to overflowing in one powerful thrust, knocking on the entrance to my womb with such force that I nearly came from the surprise of it all.

When we'd had sex in the past, it was normally slow and sensual.

This time, though, it spoke of need, want, and anger.

Fuck, I thought as he started to move. *He feels fucking divine taking up every inch of me.*

I felt heat rushing to my core, pooling pleasantly in my belly, waiting for the right moment to spill over.

A particularly hard thrust had my eyes, which I hadn't been aware had closed, open in surprise.

I stared at him, watching his muscles flex as he took me faster and faster.

Then when he had my gaze, he moved his hand from my hip, and swept his thumb over my back entrance.

That forbidden place that I'd only dreamed about in the comfort of my dark bedroom.

I gasped, asshole puckering in response, as I pushed back against him even harder.

He didn't say it, but the promise was there.

It'd be some day. Maybe not today. Or tomorrow. But one day he'd claim every hole that belonged to me. *And I'd let him.*

With that promise in my eyes, he pressed harder, inserting his thumb in that forbidden entrance.

And I detonated.

Fucking blew into tiny little pieces.

My asshole clenched on his thumb, causing erotic tingles to shoot through my body.

His triumphant grin was the last thing I saw as my vision went dark.

Either my eyes closed, or I had lost the ability to see, because when I finally came to once again, Foster had pulled out of me and stripped the condom from his length.

He was working himself slowly.

His big fist moving over the hard length of his cock.

It looked so angry.

He looked so angry.

And when he bent down and lifted his pants over his raging erection, buttoning it, I knew that this wasn't over.

We'd have it out again later.

He left without a backwards glance, but once again , the promise was there.

And I would never know when it was coming.

CHAPTER 19

Want to piss off a woman? Just open your mouth. That usually works.
-Words of wisdom

Blake

I was still mad four hours later as we drove to Benton, Louisiana.

So mad, in fact, that I hadn't said a word to Foster in all that time.

I wasn't usually one for silent treatments, but I was fairly sure if I said a word to him, I'd probably turn into my mother, and I didn't want him to witness that.

I still wanted him to love me, after all.

Not that he'd relayed those words to me.

I hadn't either, but still.

I was a lovable woman. What was not to love?

I played with a frayed piece of my jean shorts that were at the very top of my thighs.

The seated position allowing even more of my legs to show than what was supposed to.

The shorts were short to begin with, and I would've changed, but it seemed to annoy Foster that I was wearing something so revealing.

It's not like I was showing off my ass cheeks or anything, but if I bent over, they'd be visible.

He hadn't said a word, which was two points in his favor. Especially with the way he'd left me there, against the counter after he was done with me.

I did notice how he never lost the erection our entire drive, though.

Which secretly made me happy that he was suffering.

I stared in complete shock at The Dixie Warden MC's clubhouse.

Foster hadn't even waited for me.

He'd freakin' got out of the truck and started to walk inside without even waiting to see if I'd followed.

Which pissed me off.

Really, *really* bad.

So what did I do?

Absolutely nothing.

I laid my seat back, grabbed Foster's fleece line KPD parka, and draped it over myself before I closed my eyes and went to fucking sleep.

Fuck him and his party.

***

Foster

"Where's Blake?" Viddy asked me.

Viddy was my sister-in- law.

She married Trance a few years ago and they had two beautiful children together.

A girl and a boy.

Both of which were currently playing at my feet. Or foot. They were both really interested in my new prosthesis.

"No clue. Here somewhere, I'd guess," I answered her, making a cursory effort to locate her.

I wasn't worried she'd be hurt by the men after her, though.

The party we were at had a shit ton of security, mainly in the form of off duty police officers, Marines, Army Rangers, Navy SEALS, and many, many others.

The clubhouse was also inside a ten foot razor wire lined fence that you had to have a code to get into.

And seeing as this was one of the 'family' parties, no one but the families were here, which meant there wasn't any club whores or hanger-ons allowed.

"You don't know?" Viddy asked in confusion. "You didn't bring her in here?"

I shook my head. "No. When I left her, she was giving me the silent treatment."

I was also surprised at my lack of control, which had mainly been the reason why I'd left her so abruptly.

I didn't pride myself in how I'd just treated her.

In fact, I was just plain embarrassed in myself by the way I'd acted.

"Trance!" Viddy called.

Trance, who'd been at the bar talking with Kettle, one of his fellow Dixie Wardens members, turned his head to look at his wife.

"What?" He called loudly over the crowd.

"Your brother's a dumbass!" She screamed.

I shook my head in exasperation. "You don't know that."

She turned her glare towards me as she said, "Yes I do."

"We already know he's a dumbass!" Trance bellowed.

Miller, who'd walked up behind us and snatched Trance's son, Ford, up into his arms, started laughing. "That's true. We already knew he was a dumbass."

Viddy turned her glare on me. "Go find her. Bring her to me."

I sighed, disentangled my foot from a very excited to see my 'weird robot foot' and left to find my giving-me-the-silent-treatment woman.

A woman I couldn't find fucking anywhere.

Something I found out after twenty minutes of searching for her.

That's about when I started to freak out.

She wouldn't have tried to leave, right?

The gate opens automatically from the inside.

If she'd wanted to, she could've left with incredible ease.

Rushing to my truck, I hopped inside and slammed the door.

"We're leaving already?" Blake asked tiredly.

I nearly had a heart attack.

Big bad SEAL that I was and all.

"Fuck!" I groaned. "You scared the shit out of me."

"Sorry," she whispered tiredly. "I'm sorry."

I closed my eyes and reached over the console to run my hand over her long hair. "Sorry for what? You didn't do anything wrong."

"I had a nap, and got over my snit. I never meant to compare you to David. I know you'll never be him. It's just hard to stop my mouth sometime," she whispered.

Now I felt horrible.

"You have nothing to apologize for, Blake. That was all me. I should've never left you with her," I explained. "Not to mention I was acting like a child when you said what you had to say. Which all of it happened to be true. I just don't like hearing I was wrong," I explained.

She tilted her head and kissed my wrist before asking a question that had my heart stalling in my chest, and then beating double time.

"You know I love you, right?"

I closed my eyes and felt the joy of those words burst through me.

"Yeah, I figured you did."

"That's it?" She asked laughingly.

I snorted and dug my hands underneath her, then promptly hauled her into my chest.

She straddled my legs before settling her ass down on my lap, bringing my jacket that'd been covering her with her.

She wrapped it around us both before looping her arms around my neck and pulling my face to hers for a kiss.

"And to answer your question," I said, leaning forward. "I fucking love you, too."

"Fucking good," she breathed, and then kissed me once again.

My cock, which had already been not very happy with me, started to rage once again. Ten times worse now than it had been earlier.

Each beat of my pulse had my cock throbbing with need in my pants.

Something she felt, causing her to smile.

"You want me, don't you?" She exhaled.

I squeezed her ass to keep her from rotating her hips like I knew she wanted to.

"Yeah. I always fucking want you. It's like a sickness in my brain. A disease that makes me only think of you and that hot, juicy pussy of yours," I said candidly.

She giggled and moved her hands to my belt before she started to open it, followed shortly by my pants.

Then her hot little hand was on my cock, pumping it as she stared into my eyes.

"You gonna come this time?" She asked with a grin.

I pinched her ass.

"Yeah," I hesitated. "Put me inside you."

Helping her slide her indecently short shorts and panties over, she hovered over the head of my cock before she slowly dropped down onto me.

"Oh, yeah," she groaned as I filled her up fully.

Her ass was resting on the top of my thighs as she swirled her hips around, allowing me to slip impossibly further inside of her.

"Jesus," I hissed, throwing my head back as I started to urge her to move with my hands.

She took the hint, pumping her hips up and down on my cock, faster and faster.

The security light that was above my truck turned on, but I ignored it.

Her hot pussy held me captive as she moved, thrusting forward and back until I was ready to blow.

"You have to get off. I don't have a condom on," I pleaded.

She stopped completely, and I squeezed my eyes tightly shut as I willed my released to go back into my balls.

But then her own release burst free from her.

Her muscles tightened and clenched on my over sensitized cock, coaxing my dick into giving it what it wanted.

I couldn't stop it.

It burst free of me and straight into her waiting heat.

Hot, hard pulses gushed into her, bathing her willing womb in my essence.

"Goddammit," I said, squeezing my eyes tightly shut.

"Oops," she said, smiling apologetically.

I laughed and pulled her forward. "Birth control next week, please. I don't think I can do condoms anymore."

She nodded against my face, her lips moving up and down on mine.

"Now…what do I do about the mess?"

***

She wasn't wearing panties.

Those short as fuck shorts, and she had nothing on underneath them.

Not surprisingly, my cock was just as hard now as it had been when I was inside of her in my truck.

Oh, it'd gone down momentarily, but the moment she sat her ass on my lap once we got inside, it was raging and ready to go again.

"What do you do, Blake?" Viddy asked. "I've got to say, I haven't heard much about you. Foster's pretty tight lipped."

Blake tossed me a glare over her shoulder. "Are you embarrassed of me?"

I knew she was teasing, the others, however, did not.

We were at a table with both of my brothers, and their wives, as well as a few other members of The Dixie Wardens.

"I'm a dispatcher with KPD," she answered, leaning forward to take a sip of her beer.

"So you get to talk to Foster on your shift?" Viddy asked.

Blake shook her head. "Yes and no. Most of the time I just dispatch calls to them through the computer. There are times, though, that they call in something that they're doing and I talk to him. But 'talk' is not what we really do. We're not allowed to do that over the radio."

Viddy nodded. "So you could be on the line with him in dangerous situations?"

Blake shuttered, and I gave her a reassuring squeeze.

"Yeah, I've already experienced that one. It wasn't something that I would want to repeat. *Ever*," she sighed. "But I love my job, and will keep doing it."

"Isn't your ex a cop?" Mercy asked.

She nodded at Mercy. "Yeah, he is."

She smiled at me sympathetically. "Miller told me about him. I'm sorry."

She shrugged. "It's not that big of a deal. It's something I've learned to live with. Plus, had David not cheated on me, I would've never left him, and I wouldn't be with Foster right now."

Pushing her hair over her shoulder, I ran my nose along the back of her neck, causing her to giggle.

Before another question could be thrown at Blake, Sebastian stopped at our table.

"There's a nice little note on the side of your car," Sebastian said, startling me.

Sebastian was the VP of The Dixie Wardens MC and a firefighter at the Benton Fire Department.

So a 'nice little note' probably wasn't a '*nice little note*,' but more like a threatening note. Something he didn't want Blake to know about.

"Get up and let me go with Sebastian," I said, patting her thigh.

She moved up, and my eyes zeroed in on her bare ass cheeks before I moved.

Shit.

Luckily, she sat right back down on the seat, then moved forward underneath the bar's overhang, hiding everything so I could no longer see anything naughty.

"I'll be right back," I said kissing her forehead.

She nodded, but continued talking with Mercy and Viddy while I walked outside behind Sebastian.

It didn't surprise me to find Miller and Trance at my back within moments of getting outside.

They were protective.

"What's the note say?" I asked as we walked.

Sebastian didn't say a word, only walking until we came to a stop at the passenger side door of my truck.

"How'd this happen?" I asked in a deceptively calm tone.

Inside, though, I was on fire.

My mind was reeling at the thought that I was wrong.

Earlier I'd thought that Blake had been safe. Yet, here I was being proven wrong.

"I don't know, but you bet your ass I'll find out," Sebastian promised.

"You're lucky you're with the whore. Don't you know it's illegal to fuck in public?" Miller read.

I clenched my teeth.

"How'd you not see him do this?" Miller asked, walking around the truck.

"Is that…is that jizz?" Trace asked, shining the flashlight from his pocket onto the piece of paper.

"Fucking motherfucker," I growled.

Goddammit!

"He stuck his fucking note to my door with his own goddamn jizz?" I yelled, my arms waving wildly. "Pull your fucking tapes."

Sebastian grunted and we followed him, but he stopped at the entrance to the clubhouse, speaking lowly with the prospect. "Get that note into a Ziplock bag from the kitchen. Use gloves. Then wash the truck off. Yeah?"

The prospect nodded. "Yeah."

Twenty minutes later found us reviewing the tapes.

"That's Manny's brother," Trance said, looking closer.

"Manny's brother?" I asked.

Trance nodded. "Yeah. He's a member's brother. A prospect right now."

"Go get him," Sebastian said.

Trance left, and came back a minute later with a very confused looking Manny.

"What's going on?" Manny asked.

"Your brother. Where is he?" Sebastian asked.

"He said he got called into work," Manny explained.

"Where does he work?"

That's when he rocked my fucking world.

"Kilgore Police Department."

My mind blanked, and I knew instantly what I had to do.

"What's his name?" I demanded shortly.

Manny blinked. "Quentin Ortiz."

I closed my eyes, pissed off that I knew the fucker.

He worked in evidence.

"Who you calling?" Trance asked when I moved to withdraw my phone from my pocket.

I only said one word.

"Shank."

"And what's he going to do?" Trance asked.

I laughed humorlessly. "*Find him.*"

CHAPTER 20

Snugglefuck- a type of foreplay that begins with snuggling, but transforms to sex after the snuggling faze is over.
-Word of the day

Blake

I knew as soon as Foster disappeared outside that something was wrong.

I also knew that the moment he showed back up inside that something was *seriously* wrong.

Then he'd disappeared into an office, and hadn't come out since.

"Some party this is," I muttered, seeing only the women left.

The men had disappeared slowly but surely, leaving only the women.

"This happens sometimes. They're all busybodies," Viddy explained. "They can't stand to be left out of the action."

A woman whom I'd just met named Baylee, laughed.

Baylee was apparently the sister of Luke, and the wife of the man who'd been the one to call Foster outside.

She was very pretty, and had a great personality.

I could see why someone would be attracted to her.

Hell. I was attracted to her.

Only in a friendly way, of course.

"Well, I guess I should get used to it, eh? I still get kind of freaked when he catches a SWAT call, though. My daddy's a cop, too. However, he never gets called out like Foster does," I explained.

"Who's your dad?" Baylee asked. "I actually work for the Kilgore Fire Department. I'm just wondering if I've seen him around anywhere."

I smiled at her. "He's a state trooper. His name is Lou Rhodes."

She looked at me oddly. "Is he the one that saved that little baby from being kidnapped two years ago?"

I smiled fondly at the memory. "Yeah, that's him. The baby's three now, and the sweetest thing ever. He actually lives just down the street from my father."

"What happened?" Mercy asked.

I leaned back in my chair and relayed the events that had led up to the kidnapping.

"The parents were young. Maybe sixteen and seventeen, at most," I said, taking a sip of my coke before continuing. "They'd been swinging the child on the swing when there'd been a commotion in the parking lot. Some kid had ran out in front of a car, and the car swerved, hitting the bathroom that was set up for the kids. Anyway, while the parents moved to see what was going on, a man had come out from behind the slide and had taken the child when they weren't looking, taking off with him into the woods."

They all nodded, captivated with my story of my father.

"Was your dad the hiker?" Baylee asked.

I nodded.

"Yeah, he was on my uncle's land about ten miles from there. He'd been walking along the creek when he heard a baby crying and decided to follow the sound," I explained. "He found the man trying to bury the kid alive. He knocked the man upside the head with a tree branch and rescued the child. They later found out that that wasn't the man's first time to do something like that. Apparently, it was his fifth. And that was where he'd buried those children he'd abducted."

Baylee's mouth was open in surprise. "I don't remember hearing anything about that part of it."

I shrugged. "It wasn't something they shared with anybody but the parents of the deceased. It was on military property. Something my father got a fine for trespassing on. Which he later got a commendation for by his department."

"Wow!" Viddy exclaimed. "That's pretty amazing. What a relief to have an end for those parent's, too."

I nodded. "He was pretty shaken up about that. I don't think he's gotten over it two years later, either."

Just as Viddy was about to reply, she squeaked and launched herself from the booth. "Shit, Kosher. You scared the fuck out of me."

Surprised, I looked at her for a few long seconds before bending down to peer under the table.

That's when I came nose to snout with a very large dog.

"Oh, he's freakin' beautiful," I whispered, pulling a fry off my plate and offering the dog some food.

"Don't feed him. He'll get fat," an amused male voice said in front of me.

Trance.

God, his eyes!

They were freaking beautiful. One blue, and one green.

He was handsome, of course, but his eyes were what made all the difference.

I could see why he was named Trance by the MC. Something Foster had told me during the various discussions we'd had about his family.

"I don't know what you're talking about," I hedged, sneaking Kosher another fry.

He licked the fry from my hand, then swallowed it whole.

"Uh huh," he agreed. "I can see that."

I grinned unrepentantly at him. "Where's Foster?"

He pointed to a room beyond the bar. "Something came up. I was sent in here to take you ladies home with me for a while. You can meet the puppies."

"Puppies?" Mercy and I chirped at the same time.

We'd both done amazingly well about not hinting about wanting to know what was going on. It would be a losing battle. Something we both knew we wouldn't be winning wholly for the fact that if Trance had wanted us to know, he'd have told us. Instead, he'd cleanly glossed over the two men having 'something to do,' and had told us what we were doing. And I was fairly sure he wouldn't take no for an answer.

Sighing, I said, "I'll go with you on one condition."

He raised his brow at me. "What's that?"

I grinned.

***

"I want the white one," Mercy said from her perch on the floor next to me.

Oakley, Trance's daughter, picked up the white one and gave her to Mercy. "This one's daddy's favorite. You can't have her. You can have him, though."

She pointed at the other white one. The one Trance's son, Ford, was currently torturing...I mean holding.

188

"Your husband won't let you have another one," Trance drawled from his spot on the couch.

He was scratching Tequila's head.

Tequila was the mother of the massive brood. She was also a trained K-9 officer, but Trance had never used her in the field.

Kosher was the father of the brood, and surprisingly protective of them all.

"How much longer do they need to stay with Tequila before they're ready to be weaned?" Mercy asked, totally disregarding Trance's comment.

"They were ready a week and a half ago, but Viddy here seems to think that we're keeping them all, which we most definitely are not," he said, directing that comment at his wife who was sitting on the chair beside her husband.

Viddy shot him a look. "It's not that I want to keep them, it's just that I want them to have really good homes. Homes that I can visit whenever I want to so I can check on them. Make sure they're happy."

I understood that.

Although I'd heard about the retired K-9 officer dying a year or two ago, I never connected them with anyone I knew until Viddy had mentioned it upon arriving at their home.

"So I can pawn them off on my brothers, make them pay, and you're happy?" Trance asked hopefully.

She considered it for a moment, and when she didn't find any problems with it, she answered simply. "Yes."

He jumped off his chair. "Sold!"

Viddy laughed as I looked down at the puppy in my lap.

I currently had the brute of the bunch.

Trance and Viddy said that Ford had started calling him Morris, and I had to laugh.

"I have a bird named Boris. They'd be best friends," I cooed, petting the beautiful black and brown puppy in my lap.

He seriously was the most adorable thing I'd ever seen.

"You have a bird?" Trance asked in disgust. "Aren't they gross?"

I shook my head. "Surprisingly, no. He is annoying, though."

"He says, 'boom goes the dynamite' when we fuck," Foster drawled from the doorway.

I gasped, covering the closest child's ears, which happened to be Ford. "Watch your mouth!"

He grinned. "I'm sure he's heard worse."

Trance snorted, not saying a word. Viddy, though, glared at her brother in law.

Grinning deviously at Foster, she turned her evil smile to me. "So Blake…did you know that Foster hates hearing the sound of a nail file? And his feet are ticklish? Oh, he's afraid of heights, yet he doesn't like to admit it. Or…*mmmmppph.*"

Foster covered her mouth. "Remember, sister dearest. I know things about you, too. I'm sure Trance would love to know what you got him for his birthday."

"You wouldn't," she glared.

He grinned deviously. "Try me."

She opened her mouth to, what I'd guess was, blast him, but she closed it with a snap. "To answer your earlier question, Blake. Yes, you can have the dog."

"No, she can't," Foster tried.

"Why not?" I asked.

He scowled. "Because the apartment doesn't allow pets."

I could tell he was lying.

"Actually, Downy had Mocha there for months before he moved out. I'm pretty sure they won't mind," Miller said, coming into the kitchen with a beer for each of the brothers.

Foster punched Miller in the arm, making him rock back on his feet and laugh.

I smiled, enjoying the way the brothers teased each other.

I never had anything like that.

My parents had had another child a few years after I was born, but he'd been born stillborn. Something that had torn both of my parents up so badly that they never tried to have any more.

I looked down at the puppy in my arms. "Do you want to come home with me, Morris?"

"No! His name isn't Morris anymore! It's Molder!" Ford yelled loudly.

I blinked. "So it's okay if I take Molder home with me?" I asked the little boy.

He studied me for a moment. "Yeah, I guess."

Viddy giggled, slapping her husband on the arm. "That's you coming out in him."

He shrugged. "At least that's a somewhat good thing. He's got your temper, though."

Viddy smiled widely at her husband. "That's true."

"Trance, did mom tell you she was coming in in two weeks?" Miller asked, taking a seat on the floor beside his wife.

Trance shook his head. "No. Why?"

Foster took a seat on the couch directly behind me, and moved me until I was leaning against his legs.

"She said she had some news and that she wanted to tell us about it in person," Foster said, scratching 'Molder's' head.

"Are you sure you want a dog?" Foster whispered, interrupting the conversation I was listening to.

I nodded. "I've always wanted a dog. He's cute, too."

He sighed and pulled my hair backward until I looked up at him.

"You know that they shit and piss, and all that fun stuff, right?" he confirmed.

I nodded. "Yeah. I'll ask Uncle Darren if I can bring him to work with me, and keep him in his office."

He snorted. "Yeah, I'm sure that'll go over well."

***

Later that night

"No. No dogs in the station," Uncle Darren declared loudly through the phone.

I laughed. "Downy has a dog."

"Downy's dog is a trained police dog. Yours still doesn't have control of his bladder. No. Not happening," he confirmed.

"He's coming with me. I'll buy him a crate and everything," I declared firmly.

It was my uncle's turn to laugh. "You're not special. I don't allow anybody else's dogs there. Why should I allow yours?"

I grinned, knowing I had him. "Because I'm your only niece and you love me?"

He sighed. "The first complaint I have about him, he's gone. Understand?"

I hung up a happy woman.

"You're so bad," Foster said from the bed.

He was lying on his back, both hands propping his head up as he watched the ten o'clock news on the TV in front of him.

I took a freshly bathed Molder to the bathroom, and closed him in.

He laid right down on the bathmat, practically flopping down with a sigh.

"Yes, yes I am," I agreed as I crawled onto the bed.

I didn't stop on what I'd come to call 'my side' though. Instead crawling to Foster's side, and depositing myself on his lap. Legs settling on either side of his legs.

"Tell me what's going on," I ordered, knowing I'd waited long enough.

He sighed and flipped off the TV with the TV changer before tossing it on the bedside table next him.

His hands settled on either side of my hips as he looked into my eyes.

God, he was so handsome.

His normally curly blonde hair was less curly, most likely because he'd spent a lot of time running his fingers through it. Something he did when he got worried or mad.

"We think we found the man responsible for shooting up your house," he said finally.

I blinked. "How?"

He squeezed my hips slightly as he replayed something in his head.

His eyes went hard, but his voice went softer.

"There was a note on my truck door," he finally said. "We pulled the camera's feed from outside, and found him. He was a brother of one of the men with The Dixie Wardens. A new member that had transferred down here form the Alabama chapter," he explained.

"Okay," I said. "So did you find him yet?"

He shook his head. "No. But I have someone on it. As soon as he finds him, he'll let us know."

I studied his face. Noting the slight crookedness of his nose, and the way he clenched and unclenched his teeth as he waited for what I had to say next.

"Should I be worried?" I asked.

He closed his eyes. "I'd like to say no. However, I'm not going to give you false hope. You need to be vigilant and make sure you're never alone. But that's also not saying that I can't keep you safe. Which I'll do. Okay?"

I nodded. "Okay."

I knew he would, too. With his life.

CHAPTER 21

Daddies are protectors for life. Down to the very end.
-Words of wisdom

Foster

"What do you mean you haven't found him yet?" I asked.

I was probably crazy as fuck for yelling at Lou "The Shank" Rhodes, but I couldn't fucking help it.

"He's hiding. He hasn't been at his house in four days, and he hasn't been to work in the same," Lou growled.

I knew it wasn't any easier for him, but there was only so much patience to be had.

"Silas is running his name through whatever database he uses. Gabe hasn't found a damn thing on him other than his exemplary service record," I growled.

Apparently Quentin Ortiz was lucky as fuck. He'd managed to slip out of every single place we'd been able to locate the last four days.

His brother was willing to help, and had given all the known addresses he could find to us, practically throwing his brother under the bus.

Apparently, Manny and Quentin didn't get along all that well, and it showed.

Beep.

"Ahh, hold on, Lou. Manny's calling me," I said.

"Just call me back," he said before hanging up.

I rolled my eyes and switched the line over.

"Hello?" I answered.

"He has a woman…or had a woman," he said. "I remembered her last night. He used to talk about visiting her all the time before he got hurt and stuck in evidence. Her name's like Cherry…or Mary or something."

I winced. "Do you know where she lives?"

"From what I can remember it was off Fifth Street. I'm driving that way now."

"Good," I said. "I'll meet you at the Exxon at the corner."

"Got it. See you in twenty."

Swinging my cruiser around, I headed to the Exxon that was less than five minutes from my location.

Manny showed in the twenty he'd said he would, pulling up to my car opposite of me so we could talk through the window.

"I'll point it out to you if I can," he said.

I nodded, and followed him.

It didn't take long for him to find it.

In fact, it was the fourth house we passed.

He stopped, pulling over, and got out.

I did the same, meeting him in the middle of the sidewalk, both of us looking up at the simple yellow house.

It was nothing special, really.

Just a plain one story house in the historical district of Kilgore.

Expensive to rent and more expensive to own.

"This it?" I asked.

He nodded. "This is it."

Nodding, I picked up my phone and placed a call.

"I need you to run a check on something for me," I said to Gabe.

"Shoot," he said, fingers clicking on a computer.

"Address is 623 Fifth Street. Can you tell me who used to live there? Probably moved in the last year, because the neighbors think the woman left around that time," I explained.

The keyboard continued to click as I waited impatiently for the results.

Then I was stunned.

"Berri Aleo was the most recent tenant."

Mother. Fucker.

***

Shank

"You're telling me that that weasel dick of an ex of hers did this?" I asked carefully for clarification.

My hand clenched as Foster began to explain.

"The house where Manny used to be seen was last rented by Berri Aleo. David's new fiancé. The same one he cheated on Blake with," Foster clarified.

I squeezed my eyes tightly shut, sickened beyond belief that someone that'd promised to love and protect my child, my little girl, had so little regard for her that he could do something like this.

It may have been only by association, but it was still because of him that it'd happened at all.

"What else has your man found?" I asked, standing up to gather my things that I would need.

"Newest address listed as living with a one David Dewitt. Also has a rental apartment on South Tenth Street," he answered. "I'm on the way there now."

"No, you are not. You don't need to have anything to do with this. Back off." I ordered.

"You can't order me to do anything," Foster argued.

I laughed.

Watch me.

Hanging up, the next call was made to my brother.

"Hello?" Darren answered on the fourth ring.

"I need you to call in the SWAT team. Now."

CHAPTER 22

My heart bleeds as I think about losing the man that I compared
all my potential husband's to.
-Blake

Foster

I was livid.

Shank had had me pulled into a fucking meeting, and there was not a damn thing I could do about it. Not if I wanted to keep my job.

Chief Rhodes had been careful to let me know that before hanging up, having called me personally.

I stomped into the Chief's office, livid that I was here when I should be somewhere else.

"What's going on?" I asked darkly.

The Chief looked up, and sat back in his computer chair.

"What'd you do to piss him off?"

I shook my head. "Not a damn fucking thing. I found a lead on Quentin Ortiz. He told me to stay away. And made sure I did."

"He what?" He asked, jackknifing up from his chair and standing up.

I nodded. "Yeah, I found him. Or might have. He's staying at an apartment owned by the stupid cunt David Dewitt's marrying."

The chief growled in frustration.

"Get the team and go. Now," the Chief ordered.

I followed his directions, going to the war room, finding all of the men suited up and ready to go.

"What the fuck is going on?" Luke asked in frustration. "John says there's been no call."

Then the dispatcher's voice, the one who worked with Blake, came over our radios. "Code 11. I repeat Code 11. 5211 South Tenth Street. Neighbors report shots fired and a police officer on scene being dragged through the front door."

We moved as one.

I grabbed my clothes on the way out, changing in the back of Rita before we arrived on scene.

While I was doing so, I gave them a rundown of what I'd found so far.

"So, you have no idea what we're going into, do you?" Bennett asked.

I shook my head. "No. Not a single idea."

"John," Luke said into his radio. "Tell me what you got."

John was our computer man.

He could accomplish damn near anything with a computer, as long as it was under the letter of the law. Which was why I'd not brought him in on what I was having Gabe do for me.

He could've just as easily found the information out as well, but I didn't want to bring anybody into it and have it turn sour. Something I expected would be the outcome of this day if we weren't' careful.

***

Shank

"You're going to die," I smiled.

I knew I was about to die myself, but it made me feel better to know he'd be going down with me.

Karma's a bitch, motherfucker.

But I couldn't get over the fact that I'd done something so monumentally stupid.

In my head I was the badass that everyone thought I was, but in reality I was a pissed off man trying to protect his daughter. A man that knew better than to enter a volatile situation without any foreword planning.

I'd fucked up.

And now my daughter would forever think this was her fault.

Which was why I did the next stupid thing I did.

I called 911 on my cell phone. Doing exactly what the little pecker head wanted me to do.

I wanted to make sure the bastard paid. He needed to go down, and I'd make sure he did if it was the last thing I did.

***

Foster

"911 call came in a minute ago just like you said it would," John confirmed. "Managed to get Pauline to take the call. Blake knows it's her dad, though. He says he was taken hostage, and the man is making him place the call."

I swallowed the bile that formed in my throat as I thought of her having to listen to her father calling in.

Goddammit, I was so stupid. Never in a million years would I have thought Lou would go off halfcocked as he'd done, otherwise I would've never told him.

Never.

And I just got my future wife's father killed, and there wasn't a damn thing I could do about it.

"Have you pulled the blue prints of the apartment, yet?" Luke asked John.

"They're on their way to your computer right now. The bottom half of the building is under construction. So you won't have to worry about the elevator. Only one set of stairs, and two apartments on the second level. He's the first door. Second door is occupied, but the tenant isn't there. The police have him behind the police line," John explained.

"10-4," Luke confirmed. "Going black now."

We all took the stairs, two at a time, eyes trained in front and behind us.

Luke and I were at the top, Miller and Michael behind us, then Bennett and Nico

"James," Luke said once we reached the top. "You got any eyes?"

"Negative," James answered immediately. "Blinds are pulled. Not to mention the glass is covered in what looks like fake snow. I've got nothing."

"Fuck," Luke sighed. "Alright boys. Let's move."

Luke signaled with his hands, and I dropped my shotgun over my shoulder, the strap catching the gun just about my mid back.

Then I took what was deemed the 'door knocker' and rammed it into the entryway.

It opened like a twig snapping off of a branch.

I dropped down low to allow my fellow officers to cover me, and that's when the shooting started.

My world exploded, and the last thing I saw before the 'red haze' set in was Lou's blood spraying all over the white wall.

Except when the dust settled, and the gun that was peppering the wall above my head with bullets finally hit its end, I realized that there was wasn't anyone 'human' shooting at us. Whomever had been here had escaped. The only thing left was an AK-47 rigged to fire once the tension on the door was relieved.

Something I'd done myself when I'd knocked the door through with the *door knocker*.

All of it had been for nothing.

I ran inside, shotgun up to my cheek and pointed at the gaping hole in the floor. Most likely where Quentin Ortiz had disappeared.

Dropping down to my knees beside Lou, I dropped down until my ear was next to his mouth.

I didn't need to see his wounds to know it was serious.

It was beyond serious.

The AK-47 had nearly torn Lou in half since he'd been placed in front of the gun.

He'd fallen to the side at the last second, but it hadn't helped. Not enough, at least.

He still had at least eight rounds lodged in his belly.

"The new wife," Lou croaked. "That's where he's going to go. The new wife."

I dropped my forehead down to Lou's. "You're going to be okay."

He laughed, but started coughing before he even had the air out completely. "Don't lie. Just take care of her. Promise."

I was pushed to the side by the medics, unaware of when they'd arrived, but happy that the scene had been cleared and they had done it so fast.

"I will, Lou. I will. Now let them take care of you," I said, getting to my feet.

He looked at me. Straight through me, actually.

"I'll make it until I can say goodbye to her. Won't go until then," he croaked.

As they took him out of the room, I made a promise.

Nobody would ever know that Lou "The Shank" Rhodes wasn't actually on shift that day. All they'd know was that he'd died a hero, and I'd make damn sure of it.

***

Blake

I dropped to my knees, the strength quickly draining from my upper legs as the past twenty minutes just played on repeat over and over again in my head. Had I done all that I could? What should I do now? Did my mom know? Would she even care?

I'd just had to listen as my daddy, the man I'd looked up to for my entire life, called in his own 911 call.

I, luckily, hadn't been the one to catch the call.

It'd been Pauline.

But I'd heard the call go through, nonetheless.

It'd also been an officer distress call; which meant that while Pauline took the caller, I called in the backup and gave them real time information.

The door to dispatch was flung open, and my uncle, looking disheveled, threw himself through the open door.

He saw me there, on my knees, and immediately dropped to the floor beside me, gathering me into his arms.

"It's going to be okay, honey," he whispered. "Let's go. We can make it to the hospital in ten minutes."

"But Pauline will be by herself," I cried.

He shook his head, hauling me to my feet as he stood. "Don't worry about her. She's got the hatch tightened down. She can handle it for ten minutes until the backup arrives."

I nodded, not knowing what else to say.

Pauline looked at me as I passed, still on the line with whomever she'd been talking to for the last ten minutes.

I didn't know, and I didn't really care.

My dad was shot, and was on the way to the hospital.

I knew, though.

I knew down deep that he wasn't going to make it.

It would be a small miracle if we arrived and he was alive.

But I guess miracles did happen, because by the time I ran in the hospital doors behind Uncle Darren, and straight back to Trauma room one, he *was* alive.

But he didn't look good.

At all.

"Daddy," I breathed, looking at him.

The room surrounding him was a mess.

Nurses were slipping on my father's blood that was pouring out of his chest at an alarming rate; the doctors were trying to staunch the flow with little success.

My daddy was looking right at me.

His hand, covered in old and new blood, extended out to me.

One lone finger crooked, and a sob caught in my throat.

I went to him.

I didn't have a choice.

I'd never, ever not given him what he wanted.

"Hey," a dark, pissed off voice said. "Get her out of here."

I ignored the command, sidestepping another nurse, who slid and then fell on her ass in the blood at her feet.

I didn't let my dad's eyes go, though.

"Baby girl," he rasped.

Blood ran from his mouth, and he coughed.

My eyes started to leak, and the tears I'd been holding back by sheer force of will finally spilled over.

"Daddy," I pleaded, capturing his head with my face. "Don't leave me. Please, don't leave me."

I wasn't twenty four years old anymore. I was my daddy's baby girl. His only girl. The same little girl that used to crawl into bed with him and snuggle into his side.

The same little girl that used to go shooting with him on the weekends for some father daughter time.

The girl who asked her father to prom because her boyfriend, at the time, had come down with a stomach virus.

The girl that was supposed to have her fairytale wedding…with her father walking her down the aisle.

The breath in my lungs hitched as I heard him gasp, then the life I saw there started to dwindle.

"Give me one more hug, baby girl. I love…" Then he was gone.

"No," I cried. *"Please. Fix him!"*

It came out shrill, and devastated.

Everything that I was feeling in that moment was pushed into my words, and I knew I wasn't being rational. No one could survive what he had gone through.

"Time of death 0202," a saddened male voice said above me.

"Daddy," I whispered. "God. Please don't leave. *Please.*"

My voice was hoarse by the time I felt hands curl around my upper arms.

Then I turned to see Foster, dressed out fully in his SWAT uniform, even the hood still partially covering his beautiful face, standing behind me.

His eyes, though. Those were haunted. Devastated. Gutted.

"Foster," I cried softly. "He's gone."

"I know, baby girl. I know," he said.

"Do you want to donate his organs?" A brave female voice asked from in front of me.

I looked up into the eyes of a small woman with dark black hair the color of ash.

I nodded, knowing that was exactly what he'd wanted. "Yes."

Then they took him away, and I lost it.

I'd never hear him call me baby girl ever again either.

Never again.

Never.

Ever.

CHAPTER 23

They say time heals all wounds...well those fuckers can suck it.
Time doesn't heal nothing. Only Jack Daniels does.
-Note to self

The funeral of Officer Louis 'Shank' Rhodes

Three days later

Blake

I had a rose in my hand, and I plucked the petals, one by one, as I listened to my Uncle Darren give a speech about what a difference my father made in his life.

It was a good one.

A really good one.

But I knew if I listened, if I actually became invested in the speech like others around me were doing, that I'd crumble.

I'd fall to my knees and start wailing like a child.

I knew I couldn't do that.

Not in front of this many people.

Oh, they'd understand, but I'd never forgive myself.

I just had to be strong. Just had to get through the next three hours, and then I could go home. I could curl into Foster's arms, and cry myself to sleep like I'd done the last two nights in a row.

The stupid knot, the one that'd been there for days, started to widen as my uncle walked down the stairs and moved straight to my father's coffin.

The coffin itself was beautiful. But you couldn't see much of it due to the American Flag that draped the coffin.

A large picture of my father in the last photo he'd ever taken. It was standing behind the coffin with a huge sash of the metals my father had collected over his career hung off the frame's corner.

I gasped.

I'd been trying so hard to keep the cry in that I'd inadvertently attracted more attention to myself.

"Baby," Foster said, pulling me into his side.

Then my tears burst free, and I cried in front of a couple thousand people.

Broke down was too small of a word.

More like broke period.

But then the funniest thing happened.

Instead *of Tears in Heaven* coming on, like I'd chosen, *I shot the Sherriff* blasted through the speakers instead.

My head snapped up, and I looked around, startled.

Finally, I found the source of the mischief.

It was the expression on the attendant's face that had my giggle escaping.

That was so like my father, controlling things all the way from heaven.

I stood up, and walked straight to the attendant who was frantically trying to change the song.

It was divine intervention, though. In my opinion, it wouldn't be changing any time soon.

Placing my hand on the man's hand that was furiously clicking the huge X at the top of the screen, I stilled his fingers and said, "It's okay. I like this song better."

He looked at me, searching my eyes, then reluctantly withdrew his hand.

Taking over the mouse, I turned down the volume instead of turning the song off completely, then made my way to the podium.

A new strength taking over my body.

As I passed my father's casket, I ran my fingers over the length of it, smiling sadly.

At his picture, I pressed a kiss to my fingers, and then laid it upon my father's cheek before climbing the stairs.

We were having the funeral at the local stadium.

There was literally nowhere big enough to hold the people that were expected to show.

And show they'd done.

Every single bleacher, fixed seat, and hill top was taken over.

Hell, there were even some on the crosswalk that ran over the street.

I took in the people.

Familiar faces, and not.

I skipped over my mother.

She was in the very back, standing next to her sister.

She was wearing all black, as if she hadn't just served my father with divorce papers only three days before he'd died.

He'd chosen me when she'd made him choose, and she'd followed through with her promise of divorce. She'd gone so far as to have it all done online, having the papers sent to my father while he'd been at work.

And I hadn't spoken to her since

Skipping over my mother's scowling form, I finally focused on Foster.

Uncle Darren and Aunt Missy on the other side of him. A space in between them where I'd been sitting only moments before.

"I wasn't going to get up here," I told the crowd, eyes roving over the many sad faces. "In fact, up until that song came on, I was fairly sure I was going to die of heartache."

I wasn't going to lie. It still hurt. Hurt so hard it was hard to breathe…but I knew I'd survive it.

If only for him, I'd be strong and say what was in my heart to make him proud of me from where he was watching over me.

I'd kick ass at life, and make him proud.

"A few days ago, I was interviewed by the local paper," I swallowed. "I really, really didn't want to talk to the reporter, but I felt that my dad's story needed to be remembered. That he deserved to be remembered."

I looked down at the podium and told them what I'd refused to tell that reporter.

"She asked me what my favorite memory was of my father, and I couldn't pick one," I swallowed. "I was lying, though. I had one. Everyone has one. But one in particular, changed the course of my life. And it only happened a few weeks ago. The last time I was able to spend with him before he was shot and killed in that shooting."

***

Foster

I held Blake's gaze as she said what she had to say next. And I knew before the words even left her mouth that they were going to gut me.

They were going to rip out my heart and stomp on it.

And I was right.

It was a good kind of hurt, though.

"I was out back, drinking a beer with my daddy as he told me that my mother had decided to leave him," she said softly.

The microphone picked up her pain, though, and radiated it through the entire stadium for all to hear.

"I asked him what the point of love was if divorce was possible after being with someone for thirty some odd years," she said, wiping a lone tear. "Then his reply to me was to pull my head out of my ass."

She burst out laughing through her tears, and I wanted nothing more than to go up there and pull her into my arms.

But I left her there to her tell the story that I knew she needed to get off her chest.

"After a moment of shocked silence, I berated my father for his bad language, and he gave it to me straight." She smiled, the corner of her lip kicking up higher than the opposite. "He said, 'Blake Boston Rhodes. I didn't raise no dumbass. You've got a man that's one bad ass son of a bitch. Even tougher than I am. You wanna know why? Because I saw the way he looked at you.'"

She'd deepened her voice, even going as far as to put a little twang into her connotations.

"After a moment of shocked silence on my part, I asked him what he meant. And his reply was, 'Honey, it doesn't take a rocket scientist. Your mother and me, we had a good time. We lived, we loved, but what we had wasn't pure like what you and that boy have. What you have will withstand the challenge of time. He'd move fucking mountains for you. All you have to do is let him in. Tell him what you want. And when he comes and asks for your hand in marriage, which I damn well know he will, I'll tell him no. Then he'll come and take you from me anyway.

That…that right there is what tells me he wants you. He doesn't care that the woman he loves is the daughter of Shank Rhodes. He cares that you're happy, and you're you. That's what he cares about. So when he asks you to be his, you'll be the smart girl I know you are, and you'll say fuckin' yes.'"

I coughed, laughing with the rest of the people in the stadium as she recounted what her father had said.

I remembered, though, what he'd said to me only one day later when I'd asked him.

"Yes. A thousand times yes. Because I know you'll treat her like she deserves. But you tell her I said no, because she needs to know I'm there to protect her if she needs it. And know I'll always be watching you, even if I'm dead and gone. I'll find a way to kick your ass from the other side of the grave, boy. Fuck up, and you'll see."

"Then he'd given me a hug, and brought me another beer where we proceeded to get drunk and celebrate him being a 'free man' as he liked to call it," she laughed. "I've never been drunk in my life, but that night, for him, I did it."

Then, as if in a freakin' movie, every single member of the SWAT team's pager started going off.

Blake's watery eyes focused on my face, and she smiled the first sincere smile I'd seen from her in days.

"And there, boys, is what my daddy lived for. The thrill of the chase, and the excitement of catching the bad guy. Don't waste time. Get out of here and be safe," she ordered quietly.

As if in a daze, I stood and, in front of thousands of people, I blew her a kiss. One in which she caught and placed upon her heart.

Love you, I mouthed.

She winked and mouthed back, *I love you, too.*

***

"Have you told her yet?" Miller asked.

I glanced up from my perch on the porch steps of the Chief's home and shook my head. "Nothing to tell."

I took a sip of my beer, which turned into more of a gulp rather than a sip when I thought about how unfair I was being.

Blake deserved to hear it all, yet I couldn't find the courage to tell her.

"There's something to tell. She needs to hear it. Shit like this," Miller shook his head. "It has a way of coming out. Every single time. Someone's going to slip, and she's going to find out what part you played in it. She's going to know that you were the one that…" I held up my hand to stop Miller's diatribe.

"I know," I sighed, rubbing my eyes the best I could with a bottle of beer in my hand. "I fucking know."

"He doesn't have to tell me anything. I already know it all," a soft, tear filled voice called from the opposite side of the railing.

Behind where we both had our backs.

She'd come around the back of the house, most likely to find a little alone time, yet she'd walked into the middle of my pity party.

Miller slapped me on the back as he passed, heading back inside to the reception that was being held in Lou's honor.

I turned around, placing both hands on the porch railing, beer bottle hanging from one finger I had looped around the lip.

"What'd he tell you?" I asked softly.

She looked stunning in black.

I just wished I hadn't had to see her in this dress so early in our relationship. She said she only wore it for funerals and that broke my heart.

Her blonde hair was half up, half down, cascading down her back in a long sheet.

Her eyes were rimmed with coal black, and her mascara, as well as eye shadow, was heavier than I'd ever seen it.

She looked just as good now as she had when we'd left the house earlier that morning.

"Everything," she whispered, looking out over the hundreds of cars that lined her uncle's street. "He told me everything…and I don't blame you. Not at all."

I closed my eyes, relieved.

So very thankful that she understood when she could've just as easily gone the other way with her opinions.

"That's good," I whispered.

She turned to me then, her heart in her eyes, and she smiled. "I love you, Foster."

She walked up to the railing and leaned up, offering her lips to me.

"Now give me a kiss before I go deal with my mother."

I obeyed, leaning down to give her a kiss.

Her lips tasted salty, as if all the salt from her tears had gathered there for me to taste.

"I love you, too."

CHAPTER 24

Sometimes the best part of my job is that the chair spins.
-E-card

Blake

"Who was on the phone?" I asked, looking plopping down on the couch next to him.

I'd just finished washing my hands from my latest attempt to throw a pot. It was the fourth time I'd screwed one up this week.

My mind was on different things, and I caught myself staring into space for long periods of time, thinking about all that had happened over the last week.

"Um…nobody. The Chief called a meeting. Wanted me to come in in an hour," he hedged, stripping his shirt off. "I'm gonna go take a quick shower."

I followed behind him, knowing he was hiding something the moment he wouldn't look me in the eye.

"What does he want to talk about?" I asked, following him into the bathroom.

He was stripping off his pants as I walked in, and my eyes were immediately caught by the newest tattoo on his side.

It was a lone flower.

A red rose, to be exact.

It was taking up his whole left side. He'd gotten it the second night after my father died, saying that the flower reminded him of me. Reminded him that he had something beautiful in his life, and he needed to keep his head on straight, even when all he wanted was to find those responsible for hurting my father.

I'd thought the sentiment was quite beautiful, and I liked looking at the tattoo; especially when I knew he'd gotten it because of me.

"Some SWAT stuff," he answered before he started removing his prosthesis.

I'd seen him do it so many times now that it was just routine, even though the entire process still enraptured me.

It simply amazed the hell out of me that he was able to adapt as he had. He acted like there wasn't a single thing wrong with his life, even though he was living with a handicap that would've debilitated some men.

Moving up until I was in between his splayed legs, I wrapped my arms around his head and pulled him to me.

He laid his head on my breasts and breathed me in, the tension in his shoulders loosened the moment I put my hands on him.

"You don't have to tell me, Foster. But don't lie, okay?" I asked softly, tilting his head up so I could see his eyes.

He winked. "Yes, ma'am."

He leaned forward and placed a soft, open mouthed kiss on my collarbone, sending shivers up my spine and straight to my nipples.

"I still think you need time," he rasped against the skin of my neck.

That was something he'd been saying to me for the past few days when I tried to get him to make love to me. He'd go just far enough that I was satisfied, but not a millimeter further.

Today, though, wouldn't end like that. He needed the release just as much as I did.

I grabbed a hold of his hair, pulling it back until I could see his eyes clearly.

"What I need," I said, running my lips down his neck to his Adam's apple. "Is to be distracted. Something you do very, *very* well."

He growled, and I felt the vibration that started on my lips all the way down to my clit.

"You don't know what you're asking," he tried, gripping my hips so hard that it was at the verge of pain.

I laughed quietly before grazing my teeth along the cord of his neck.

"I know exactly what I'm asking."

With that he snatched me forward and kissed the hell out of me.

His mouth dueled with mine while his fingers found their way to the loose waistband of my pants.

I'd yet to put on jeans…or anything that resembled presentable to wear into public, since my dad had died.

I'd felt less than sexy.

However, right now, I felt like a fucking queen.

Foster devoured my mouth, then moved to allow his beard to run along the soft skin of my neck.

Tickling and turning me on all at the same time.

I grabbed a hold of his hair when he started to lower me to the freezing cold tile lining the bathroom floor.

"Eeek!" I squealed, thrusting my bare ass up when my butt met cool tiles.

His eyes smiled as he tugged my pants the rest of the way off my legs, and then settled his naked body in between my splayed thighs.

His mouth found my neck again, traveling down the length of my t-shirt until he found the bare skin of my belly, smoothing his mouth over it languidly.

"I want to plant my baby in here," he whispered gruffly. "I want to see you growing fat with my kid so bad my heart hurts."

I laughed as he skimmed his mouth up the length of my belly until he met the underside of my left breast.

"I'll have to see what I can do about that," I breathed, gasping in a fresh gulp of air when his tongue found my nipple.

He didn't suck it, though.

He flicked it. Bit it. Pulled it.

Did everything *but* suck it. Mostly because he knew what playing with my nipples did to me, and if he started to suck, then I'd lose my ability to focus.

Something he liked to only do right when I was at the brink of orgasm.

"Please," I lifted my hips up, urging him to give me what I so desperately wanted.

He grinned, lifting up onto his knees to push his boxer briefs down his thighs.

My mouth watered at seeing his cock.

As it always did.

He really did have a perfect one.

A thick, ruddy head followed by a luscious shaft.

I wanted to worship it in my dreams it was that good.

I'd never been one to think penises were beautiful, but Foster's was just that.

I started to lean forward to capture the beauty in my mouth, but he stayed my movement with a palm to my belly.

"Stay," he ordered. "I want to look at you."

I didn't know what he saw.

I knew what I saw, though.

My t-shirt had been pushed over my breasts, just barely revealing my rosy nipples to his gaze. My bare ass was pressed against the still cold tile, I'm sure completely clashing with the dark brown mosaics.

Then there was my hair.

Up in a messy bun that hadn't been brushed in a day or two, my hair was a disaster.

Yet, Foster never once complained. He thought I was freakin' beautiful. Something he made a point to mention at least once a day. Sometimes even more.

And that, more than anything else, was what turned me on the most.

Seeing the lust in his eyes was a complete turn on, and then some.

My hand snaked from my belly down to my clit as I started to circle it with a lone finger, hoping to urge him into action with the movement.

He didn't move, though. Only watched me move faster and faster.

It was only when my hand moved to my nipple, and my eyes started to close in the beginnings of an orgasm that he finally thrust home.

It was such a surprise that I came, hard and fast.

The orgasm that had been upon me suddenly pushed me over the cliff so hard that I screamed until I became breathless.

He growled, dealing me punishing thrusts as he rode me through my orgasm.

It wasn't long until he was coming, too. Spilling himself inside of me in long, rough bursts.

"Uhhh," he groaned planting himself deep and freezing.

I wrapped my arms around his neck and my legs around his ass before pulling him towards me.

He dropped down to his forearms just above me and smiled at my sleepy, sated eyes.

"Nap time?" He grinned.

I nodded.

"Yeah, just have to find the energy to get there."

In the end, we showered together, and then he took me to bed.

I'd thought we'd both fallen asleep, yet when I woke up an hour later, his side of the bed was empty, and had been for some time.

***

"You'll let me be there," I snarled at my uncle.

I really wasn't budging on this.

After Foster had left the house so abruptly an hour before, I'd known that something was going on.

My uncle sighed and opened the door wider, allowing me into the interrogation room.

"Officer, my client has done nothing wrong. She's in a delicate condition, and would like to go home to bed, where she's supposed to be until she's further along in her pregnancy," the slimy lawyer said as I walked in the door.

Foster, who'd been standing in the corner with his eyes glued to the questioning taking place a room away, stiffened when he realized I was there.

"Blake…" he started, but stopped when I raised my hand up, halting his smooth tongue.

If the bastard thought he could fuck me and leave me sated in bed and I'd forgive him for leaving me, he had another think coming.

Mainly in the form of the silent treatment from yours truly.

"What's happened so far?" I asked my Uncle.

My arms were currently wrapped around Molder who'd, of course, accompanied me to the police station via a laughing Downy.

The man thought it was hilarious that I 'didn't obey Foster.' His words, not mine.

I just glared and refused to talk to him either.

I did think it was the cutest thing in the world when Molder started to bother the shit out of Mocha, Downy's K-9 partner.

"Sorry man," Downy said, breaking the silence. "I tried."

"Uh-huh. She's all of a hundred and thirty pounds to your two fifty. I'm sure you tried real hard," Foster drawled.

Downy shrugged and took a seat next to the other members of the SWAT team.

Why they were *ALL* there, I didn't know. Something I would've thought Foster would've told me. Especially since I'd thought it was agreed upon that he wouldn't leave me out of the loop anymore.

Regardless, though, I was here now, and I was staying until I had some answers. Answers that a certain someone wasn't giving me.

"Can you tell me why you have an apartment in your name when you've been with David here for quite a long time?" The detective asked.

"We use the apartment as storage. We had to condense both of our places down into one, and we've found it's cheaper for us to keep paying the rent since she was contracted in," David said, explaining it away perfectly.

"I actually looked into that myself," the detective said. "I kind of thought that might've been the reason. The lease on the apartment was up two months ago. The cost of 'renting' the apartment was four hundred and thirty two dollars a month, yet neither one of you had that money coming out of your accounts. Nor do either one of you withdraw any money, so if that was the case, how'd you pay for it?"

"Uh-oh, spaghetti-o!" Downy teased, snapping his fingers in rapid succession. "O'Keefe's got you, bitch!"

I looked over at him, and the crazy man had pulled out popcorn.

Where he'd pulled it out of, I didn't know. I'd probably never know.

Silly man.

"Detective," the slimy lawyer drawled lazily. "You can't prove anything. It's all circumstantial."

Detective O'Keefe smiled.

"So you didn't know that Quentin Ortiz was staying at your place?" Detective O'Keefe clarified.

David finally stood up. "Listen, O'Keefe. We both have alibis for that night. You haven't found anything…"

"When was the last time you saw Quentin Ortiz?" The detective spoke over David, directing the question at Berri.

I snorted, covering my mouth at the fuming look taking over David's usually very amiable features.

Foster's arms wrapped around me from behind, and he rested his head on the top of mine.

He didn't say a word, and neither did I.

We'd get to that later. For now, I was leaving it alone.

"She already said she didn't know anything!" David bellowed.

With that, Detective O'Keefe finally gave his full attention to the man.

"Listen here, DeWitt. I've had about all I can take of your mouth. How about you go on out of here and let me speak to your woman alone," Detective O'Keefe said.

It wasn't what he said, but *how* he said it.

"Someone go get him out of there. Bring him in here and let him watch what happens next," Foster suddenly said.

CHAPTER 25

A female that truly loves you will stick with you until the end. Your mother that is, not me. 'Cause I sure ain't dealin' with your shit anymore.
-Blake to Foster

Foster

"Get your fuckin' hands off me," David hissed, ripping his arm roughly from Luke's grip.

Luke shoved him down into a seat at the front, which meant he never saw that I was standing in the back.

David growled something unintelligible at Luke, and Luke followed it up with something low of his own. "Sit down and shut up. We're trying to fucking help a fellow fucking officer. Shut the fuck up and watch."

I blinked, surprised at the vehemence in his voice.

David's body slumped, and I was surprised at how defeated he looked.

Wow, he truly did care about her!

I'd had my doubts, but this proved to be something I never expected.

I mean, how could you care about someone that was clearly lying?

Every one of us could see it. Was he in so deep that he couldn't?

"Alright, Ms. Aleo," Detective O'Keefe sat down. "We know you were involved. It's only a matter of time before the entire thing is revealed. How about you go ahead and let us know what's going on."

"You're lying," she hissed. "You have nothing on me."

O'Keefe smiled. It was a mean smile. One that he must use solely for the interrogation of suspects.

"Your *ex-husband*, Emmett Aleo, was a very helpful man," Detective O'Keefe said, leaning back in his chair.

His posture spoke of ease and triumph.

He had her and he knew it.

"If you're not arresting my client, we're leaving," the lawyer said, standing abruptly.

O'Keefe stood, too.

Then he pulled out some papers from his back pocket.

"Your husband was very helpful, actually," he said, offering the lawyer a stack of papers.

The lawyer took it, and his head hung. "Fuck."

Well that wasn't very lawyer-like.

Foster's arms around me squeezed tightly before letting loose of me and moving closer so he could stand next to the window again.

David glared at his back, and I had to cover my mouth to hold in the laughter that threatened to boil from my throat.

"I bet he gets a confession from her in three minutes," Downy said, tossing a piece of popcorn into his mouth.

"Two."

"Five."

"Seven."

"One."

That last comment was made by Nico, which had caused David to turn around and see just who, exactly, was in the room with him.

I gave him a little wave when his eyes landed on me, causing him to glare and turn around so abruptly that his chair rocked.

The lawyer laid his papers down on the table in front of Berri, and her eyes were dragged there unwillingly.

Then her eyes widened.

"What do the papers say?" I asked no one in particular.

"Do you know what that means, Ms. Aleo?" The Detective asked.

"Just wait for it," Bennett said. "It's going to be beautiful."

I snorted, but nonetheless 'waited for it.'

Berri refused to say anything.

"Those are divorce papers," Detective O'Keefe said.

David snorted, but then froze at the detective's next words.

"Divorce papers from Quentin Ortiz," O'Keefe continued. "Tell me, Ms. Aleo. Why didn't anyone know you were married to Quentin Ortiz last week when we visited you? Maybe because nobody was supposed to know? Your *fiance* knows, though, doesn't he?"

"I guess, since you're not going to help out, you can tell me if I get anything wrong. Like I said, your ex-*husband* was very helpful," O'Keefe said cheekily. "Mr. Ortiz and you are con artists. Marry separate people, take them for all they're worth, and move on to the next one. But you stay married to each other while you do it, which is where y'all screwed up."

Berri's eyes went crazy as she tried to look for an escape.

However, there wasn't one. O'Keefe had her and we all knew it.

"Your husband plea bargained out, tossing you under the bus in exchange for lesser charges," O'Keefe said. "He was adamant, though, that you screwed up and then, in turn, screwed him over. See, you weren't supposed to get pregnant. Something you'd done with David Dewitt. And he was mad, but you convinced him this could work in your favor. That you could get more money. Except something…or someone, upset you. And you went back to your ex-husband, Quentin Ortiz, and asked him to do something for you."

She finally broke.

"I went and found them. I wanted what was rightfully mine. I'm the one having the baby. She's not. So why can't I have it?" Berri hissed.

"How'd you know he'd do it?" O'Keefe asked, arms crossing casually across his chest.

"The newspaper. With her little 'We're Heroes Too' story she got in the paper the day after it happened. I hadn't realized he was doing that sort of thing. When I leave my exes, I have no contact with them again."

"And this time?" O'Keefe asked.

"That stupid whore of an ex of David's. She refused to give me the heirloom that was rightfully mine," she snarled.

"All of this over a fucking cradle?" I half yelled. "David, you stupid son of a bitch!"

I tried to launch myself at him, but I wasn't stopped by Foster, or my uncle, but Downy.

His bowl of popcorn went tumbling out of his lap as he grabbed me around the waist before I could make it to David.

Once he had me around the waist, he practically tossed me through the air towards Foster, who then caught me and clamped his steely arms tightly around my chest.

"It's okay, honey," he whispered. "He feels horrible. Look at him."

Reluctantly, I did, and I didn't like what I saw.

He did look horrified.

He looked broken. Yet, I didn't care. Not in the least bit.

I'd lost my father, my best friend, all because David couldn't keep his stupid cock in his pants.

"I'm going home," I whispered brokenly.

"I'll come," Foster said, starting to let me go, but I shook my head.

"No," I stopped him when he would've followed. "Downy can take me. In fact, I'll go see grandpa. We'll spend some time together. You can come get me when you're done."

With that, I walked out of the door, stopping when my feet hit the popcorn bucket.

On a whim, I bent down and launched the bucket at David's head, and the cardboard bounced off before landing unceremoniously on the floor.

Snickers followed.

He looked down at his feet, avoiding eye contact, and only serving to make me even madder.

"Coward," I muttered as I stormed out of the room, and then quickly walked down the hallway.

"Slow down, Blake. I'm full. You don't want me to throw up my popcorn, do you?" Downy teased as he caught up with me.

I tossed him a look over my shoulder that spoke volumes about everything I was feeling, and he grinned.

The fucker grinned.

"You're horrible. I don't know how your woman puts up with you," I sighed, walking out the backdoor and straight to Downy's truck.

"Memphis loves me. She puts up with anything as long as I'm happy," Downy laughed.

"Whatever. Just take me to my pop's place," I ordered sullenly.

"What about your dog?" He asked.

I shrugged. "Foster can get Molder. Now just go."

"Yes, ma'am," he said with a smile in his voice. "Anything for you."

It was all fun and games, too…that is until we got to my dad's house.

The first thing that made me realize something was wrong was the fact that the garage door wasn't open.

Usually at this time of day my grandfather was out working on his car he had in the garage.

Yet the garage wasn't open, and the blinds were pulled.

Hell, even the blackout curtains were down.

"Something's wrong," I whispered as Downy pulled his truck into the driveway.

"What?" He asked, putting the truck into reverse and backing out of the driveway.

He pulled four houses down and stopped in front of Mrs. Peseta's place.

"I don't know. But there's usually activity going on. My grandfather gets up at six A.M. And doesn't close the curtains until he's ready to go to bed. Either there's something wrong with him, or…I don't know…*something*."

Downy pulled his phone out and made a call.

"I need a couple of blue and white's at 222 Sheffield. Come in priority two. Park next to my truck- a white Chevy," Downy said into his radio.

Like Foster, he had it under his dash. It must be a cop thing.

I waited and waited some more for Downy to get out and check it out, but he never did.

He just watched and listened.

"You're not going to go check it out?" I asked finally.

He glanced at me. "Not yet. I'll wait until I have someone on you before I go. I'm not leaving you by yourself."

"But…"

He stopped my next argument with just a glance of his eyes.

"Not going to happen."

My heard ached as I looked behind me, wondering if my grandfather was alright.

God, please let him be okay. I can't lose him, too.

CHAPTER 26

I know it's hard to admit that you're wrong, but I can survive
without oral sex…can you?
-Blake to Foster

Foster

Miller and Nico rode with me, while Luke, Michael, and Bennett followed closely behind.

"Tell me the layout of the house," Luke asked through the radio.

We'd switched to a confidential channel, so I felt safe telling them everything I knew.

"Three bedrooms. One large open living room and kitchen. Laundry room that leads to the garage. Back porch. Two bathrooms. One off the living room, and one in the master," I informed them. "Grandfather's room is the very back bedroom on the right. It has an entrance to the outside by a sliding glass door."

I finished the last sentence as we took the last turn that led up to Downy's truck.

We'd gone the back way so we didn't have to pass the house, therefore not drawing any undue attention to us as we came.

When we got out, I grabbed Downy's bag from the backseat and tossed it in his direction. Which he promptly caught and started to dress in his gear.

"Did you hear all that, Downy?" Luke asked as we walked up.

He nodded, turning to acknowledge his best friend and boss. "10-4."

"Detective O'Keefe's right there," I pointed the unmarked car out to Blake. "Stay with him, and don't leave him, no matter what you hear. Understand?"

She nodded, eyes brimming with tears. "Got it."

I winked at her, pulled my hood down, and started across the yard behind Luke.

"Wait!" She yelled, making me stop.

I turned on a dime and looked at her.

She ran up to me, gave me a swift kiss on the lips…well, the best she could with a mask covering my face, and started to rush back towards O'Keefe who was just getting out of his car.

"Be safe!" She ordered over her shoulder.

"Be safe, big boy!" Downy jeered, imitating Blake's voice so well that I had to look at him in surprise.

He laughed and pulled his own mask down before we started to the car.

"Okay," Luke said. "Downy you take your team to the back. The grandfather's room. My team'll take the front."

I went with Luke since I was on his unofficial team, and covered his back as we moved swiftly up the front steps.

The first thing I saw was the front door propped open.

My stomach plummeted as Luke pushed it open more.

The door swung open into the eerie silence of the living room, not making a single sound as it did.

That's when I spotted the blood.

And a lot of it.

Luke was the first one to enter, dropping down to one knee the second he entered the door.

Nico went ahead, clearing the room, followed shortly by me, taking his back.

"Clear."

"Clear."

Luke and Downy said it at the same time, allowing us both to move.

My eyes were drawn to the blood trail, a smear of it extending from the front door to the kitchen, and then even further to the garage.

I signaled to Luke, who quickly nodded, allowing me to lead the way into the garage.

I'd never know what shocked me more.

The fact that the man I'd thought had his blood soaked into the living room floor was actually standing up beating the shit out of Quentin Ortiz, or the fact that Ortiz was sitting on a stool, tied there with duct tape, getting the absolute tar beaten out of him by an eighty nine year old man.

"Holy fucking shit," I breathed, lowering my weapon once I'd cleared the room.

"Hiya," Grandpa Rhodes crowed. "Caught this little boy here breaking into my house. I'm just having a little fun with him."

The old man's voice sounded frail as he said that, but his movements as he continued to beat Ortiz up was anything but weak.

"Ummm," Luke said. "Clear."

I looked down, taking in the kiddie pool that was erected underneath the legs of the stool Ortiz was taped down to, then couldn't help the small laugh that bubbled out of my throat.

"I just…I just…what the fuck is going on?" Downy asked, flabbergasted just as we were by what he was seeing.

I snorted. "Now can you see why I gave the old goat a ticket? He's fucking insane…and a badass just like his son."

The old man laughed. "Where do you think that boy learned his skills, you dumb ox?"

He followed up that question with a punch to the gut, followed by a quick uppercut to the jaw.

"Um, Mr. Rhodes, do you mind if we take him off your hands?" Downy finally asked.

"Oh! Sure! Just let me," he got in two last hits. One in the groin, and one straight to the man's Adam's apple. "Alrighty, all finished, my boys."

He stepped back, grabbed his cane that was leaning up against the project Mustang, and hobbled slowly out of the room.

We watched him go, stunned and silent, wondering if we'd seen just what we thought we'd seen.

"Do you…am I…motherfucker. *I want to be him when I grow up*," Michael breathed.

I laughed then, so happy that the old fucker was okay that I could barely see straight.

"This is Officer Spurlock, badge number 654," I said into my mic. "Scene is clear. We'll need a bus."

***

"Look at your poor hands!" Blake cried to her grandfather for the fifth time.

We'd had Grandfather Rhodes cleared by medical personnel, then we'd taken him back to his home…even though Blake had flat out refused to leave him at home by himself.

"Listen, girl. I'm fine. I'm eighty nine, not twenty. I know how to take care of myself. Get in your godforsaken car and go home. Now," the old goat growled, practically shoving his granddaughter out the door, then slamming it in her face.

The lock slid home, and the beeping of the alarm sounded quickly after that. Followed by the slow shuffling steps of him walking away.

"I can't...I...what the fuck?" Blake sighed, shaking her head and turning on her heel to stomp to my truck. "What are you waiting for, Christmas?"

She tossed that lovely statement over her shoulder, making me want to laugh.

I managed to keep it in, though, following her to the truck, watching her ass sway as I did.

She was in the passenger seat with the door closed before I was even able to get to her, and I growled in frustration before getting into the driver's side and starting the truck up.

"He'll be okay," I said soothingly.

She snorted. "I know that. The old goat is too persistent to die. I love the shit out of him, but sometimes he's so stubborn and pigheaded."

I tossed her a look, and stifled the urge to laugh once again. "And you're not?"

She shook her head vehemently. "Absolutely not. I'm freakin' perfect."

I drove the three blocks to the apartment building and pulled into a front row parking spot, shutting off the engine the moment I was close enough to the curb.

"You know..." she hesitated, looking over at me. "There's no reason for me to stay with you anymore. I'm safe. You've caught the bad guys. You could probably take me home...if you wanted."

I ignored her idiotic statement, and instead got out, slamming the door behind me.

I was halfway up the steps to my apartment when her indignant growl of frustration followed me up the stairs.

"You're a stubborn..." she climbed the steps, huffing and puffing the whole way. "Infuriating, butthead, annoying...*you did not just close that door in my face!*"

I had to laugh when she threw the door open.

"Welcome, welcome," the bird crowed. "Molder, you pecker head."

Did I mention her bird was annoying?

And a tattletale?

I'd made it into the bedroom after letting the dog out, and was in bed removing my prosthesis when she finally came in, Molder in her arms.

She glared at me as she dropped the beast in the bathroom, and closed the door behind him.

"You know what your problem is?" She asked, yanking the shirt off her body.

Her boobs popped free of her bra with the force of it, and my eyes immediately zeroed in.

"Hmm?" I asked, licking my lips at the sight.

Jesus, no control, Spurlock! Get your head in the game!

"What's my problem?" I asked.

She narrowed her eyes at me when I finally bothered to look up.

"Your problem," she said, stripping her jeans from her hips. "Is that you never take me seriously. I tell you something, and it goes in one ear and out the other. Is that something I have to look forward to for the rest of my life? Because I don't think I can handle any more dumb men."

My heart skidded to a stop, and then started pounding double time.

"You want to spend the rest of your life with me?" I asked, clarifying.

"There you go being dumb again," she snapped, pulling her bra over her head and tossing it to the floor.

Her breasts bounced, and the day…the fighting...everything, flew out the fucking window.

All I knew was that I was taking her.

Right fucking then.

I leaned forward, snaked my hands around her waist, and practically ripped her panties from her legs.

Then I leaned back on the bed, jerked her up until she was straddling my face, and started to feast on her pussy.

Instantly, she was wet for me. So wet that she was practically pouring her essence into my mouth.

"Mmmm," I growled against her lower lips.

I could feel my beard getting wet with her juices, and shook my chin to dig my tongue deep inside her.

"Oh, my God," she breathed, her thighs clenching my head as I ate her.

Her hands went to my hair as she started to rock on my face, working herself into a rhythm that would quickly have her barreling towards her orgasm.

Before she could get too far, though, I quickly switched our positions, flipping her over onto her back and yanking her down the bed in one swift motion.

I jerkily yanked my cock out of my underwear, lined it up with her entrance, and thrust roughly inside of her.

I started to move, finding the fact that I was only standing on one leg the least of my worries as her pussy took me up to the hilt.

The way her sheath surrounded my dick was like fucking magic. Vagina magic that really had all the power in the world.

Something that could bring me to my knees easily if I let her. And boy did I.

"Foster," she breathed, thrusting her hips up.

Not wanting her to have any leverage or control of the situation at all, I moved until only half of her back was on the bed, the rest of her being supported by my upper body alone.

Except then I found myself not having leverage myself, and fell backwards.

Blake let out a short scream as she fell from the bed with me, both of us landing on the floor in a heap.

My cock, however, was safe.

"Next time, don't take that thing off when you plan to go all he-man on me, okay?" She asked, rolling me until she was straddling my hips.

I held the base of my cock and pointed it straight in the air, groaning incoherently when she sank down. Her pussy magic taking hold of me once more.

"Yes ma'am," I managed to get out, urging her to move faster by placing both of my hands on her hips.

She giggled, but complied with my urging, riding me fast and hard.

The orgasm that I felt gathering in my balls earlier started to boil up my spine once again.

"Play with yourself," I ordered her, watching as she did so.

Her hand went down, dipping down to touch the base of my cock as she moved up, gathering her juices.

Then she dragged those fingers up to her clit, and started making quick, frantic circles.

"Yes," she said, throwing her head back.

I squeezed my eyes tightly shut, the muscles in my belly tensing when she started to contract around me.

Then she let out a strangled scream and ground her pussy down into me. Hard.

"Oh, Goddammit. Your pussy. Ugh," I growled, jackknifing up until I was sitting up.

She laughed breathlessly as I started slamming her down onto me, breath leaving both of us in a rush as I finally came, cutting off both of our air supplies when I slammed my mouth down onto hers.

My come left my cock in a rush, spurting into her tight sheath so hard that I thought my spine had ripped out right along with it.

After our movements became less frantic, she raised her mouth from mine, and looked me in the eyes as she said, "See? Dumb."

I leaned forward and nipped her lip with my teeth.

"Yeah, yeah," I said, slapping her ass then squeezing it tightly. "I don't see you complaining, though."

She glared. "Yet. You don't see me complaining, yet."

CHAPTER 27

The most deadly mammal on the planet is a silent, smiling woman.
-Note to self

Blake

1 month later

"What is it?" I asked Foster with a smile.

He pushed the box closer to me until it touched the tips of my knees.
"Just open it."

I narrowed my eyes at him, looking around the living room with my
family surrounding me, and smiled.

It was a genuine smile.

Not one of the fake ones I'd been trying to pass off as real ones.

Everything was finished.

The people who'd been involved with the shooting of my father were
caught, and I was free to live my life.

Although it didn't necessarily feel right still, because a day never passed
that I didn't want to tell my father something.

"Just open it. I promise you'll like it," he said in exasperation.

Grabbing the knife he was holding out to me, I split the tape open and
slowly opened the box.

Whatever was in it was wrapped in hot pink tissue paper, making it
impossible for me to see what it was.

Standing, I bent over the huge box and unwrapped the paper.

The first thing I saw was the Texas State Trooper emblem on the front of blue fabric.

Looking at Foster sharply, I reached inside the box and took out what looked to be a blanket.

But I caught the very edge of it, which enabled the fabric to unfold itself, revealing the beauty inside.

"Ohh," I breathed, tears immediately stinging my eyes as I took it all in. "Oh, my God, Foster."

Turning to him with tears in my eyes, I threw myself at him.

"It's beautiful," I declared loudly through my tears.

Foster's mother took the fabric from my hands and held one end out to Miller.

"Here, dear. Hold this so she can see it."

I turned as a sob caught in my throat. "Oh, Foster."

It was a quilt of epic proportions.

King sized, most likely, and it was made of t-shirts. All of them my fathers.

Uniforms, his favorite shirts, even what looked to be pieces of his bullet proof vest.

"Oh," I cried. "God, it's so beautiful."

I may have been a tad bit emotional, but it was the best present I'd ever received.

I walked forward, trailing my hand along the direct middle square.

It was my dad's uniform. The one I saw him in every other day for the entirety of my life.

The patch above his heard declaring him a Texas State Trooper, was absolutely stunning.

Then there was the t-shirt we got from Sea World when I was fifteen, when the dolphin sprayed him with a mouthful of water.

Or the one from Destin, Florida where I made him get a spray painted t-shirt of a turtle.

That had been one my favorites.

My dad had always been a pretty fun guy. Not caring in the least about what anyone thought. He only cared that his daughter was happy.

Then I got to the very last one.

The shirt that I'd last seen him in.

It was a simple faded black tee, but it meant the world to me.

I'd cried on my dad's shoulder, and he'd hugged me and told me he loved me.

Forever that would be in my memories. Especially now that Foster had gotten me such a beautiful memento of my father.

I turned to him, but he wasn't where I was expecting him to be.

Instead, he was on the floor, down on one knee.

He had a small velvet box in his hand, and he was looking at me with his heart in his eyes.

He had yet to strip out of his uniform, so his clothes were still stained with dirt and debris from what I could only assume was a scuffle, but would never have the guts to ask because I honestly didn't want to know.

As long as he came home safe at night, I wouldn't be asking. It was better not knowing.

If he wanted to talk about it would be a different story.

I'd always listen. For him, I'd do anything.

"My eyes are up here, sweetheart," Foster teased, drawing my eyes from the floor to his face.

I grinned. "Yeah, I know. I was debating on whether or not I wanted to ask you what you did to get so dirty."

He winked. "A misunderstanding."

"What's that you got there?" I asked, a smile overtaking my face.

He flipped it open, and my breath caught.

"It's pink!" I said laughingly.

He grinned. "Yeah, I know. I searched high and low for this, and I think I came up with a winner."

I was practically bouncing on my feet at this point, so happy I could barely contain the squeal of excitement.

"Well?" I asked when he took too long to ask the question.

"Don't hurry me, woman. I'm trying to ask you to marry me. I just have to figure out what I was planning to say," he snapped.

"Yes!" I said exuberantly. "Yes! Let's do it now!"

He scowled at me. "I had this all planned."

I shut my mouth, eyes going wide as I waited for him to get on with it.

He sighed, and stood. "There's no reason to do it now. Put it on."

I snatched the box away from him, grabbing the bright pink ring from him.

It wasn't the normal engagement ring, but the man knew me like the back of his hand.

He knew I didn't like jewelry. So he chose to give me something he knew I would like.

I'd showed him the things jokingly when I saw it on a website, but he'd taken it to heart, and remembered every word I'd said.

"You remembered," I whispered, fitting the rubber ring on my finger. "It fits perfectly."

He winked. "I listen…sometimes."

"Isn't that made for weightlifters or something?" Mercy asked as she came up to us to look at the ring.

I held out my hand to her. "Yeah, it is. But it's more for an active person. I may not be as active as I used to be, but it'd be perfect if I decided to be the girl version of Arnold Schwarzenegger."

Foster choked on his beer that he'd just put to his lips. "You will not become the girl version of him. I'll have to leave if you ever do. There's no way I can fuc- ow! I was just teasing! But really, there's no way I'd be able to sleep with someone like that. I'd be too afraid they'd whip out a dick bigger than mine."

Foster's mom raised her hand for another go around, but switched targets at the next thing that came out of Miller's mouth, hitting him directly upside the head.

"That wouldn't be hard to do," Miller snickered as he twisted away from the blow.

Foster stomped down with his blade, taking out the toes of Miller's foot, causing him to scream. "Goddammit! I knew when you did that the other day it wasn't on accident! That foot thing hurts!"

Sloan wrapped me in her arms. "Welcome to the family, baby!"

I hugged her back. "Thank you."

"I haven't heard yes yet. Have you heard yes yet, dad?" Miller asked loudly.

Foster glared, and I grinned.

"I haven't heard a definite yes, yet," Micah confirmed.

I winked and walked up to Foster, throwing my arms around his shoulders. "Do you even need to hear the yes? I'll give it to you if you do."

He wrapped his arm around my waist, pulling me in until I was knees to chest with his. "I think I can figure out that you want my body."

My face turned a deep scarlet red, and I pinched him on the shoulder. "Shut up!"

He grinned unrepentantly, and then swung me around in a circle. "Now," he said. "What are you making me for dinner, woman?"

I flipped him off and was about to reply when the phone rang.

Foster broke off to answer it, and I went back to admiring the quilt he'd had made.

It really was awesome.

And I would love it forever.

"Umm, sure. Hold on just a moment," Foster said weirdly, causing me to look up. "It's for you."

He held the phone out to me, and warily, I took it.

"Hello?" I answered.

"Um, hi. This…you don't know me. But I know you. And I'd like to meet you," a woman's hesitant voice said softly.

CHAPTER 28

Take a deep breath, you're home now.
-Coffee Cup

Foster

I walked behind Blake, hesitant to let this happen.

I knew it was all very innocent, but I didn't want her to freak out.

After doing a little digging, I found out just what the woman on the phone had wanted, and if I was right, it was going to make Blake cry. *And I hated seeing her cry!*

But I knew she'd want to do it, at least in the long run. So I didn't tell her what and who she was meeting.

"Do you think that's them?" Blake whispered at my side.

I followed her finger to the corner where a very beautiful young woman, and a little boy were playing in the corner.

"She said she'd be sitting in the corner and she'd be wearing red. I assume that's her. The little boy that she said would be there is there too."

"It's her, honey. Go over there and talk to her," I urged, giving her a slight push on the back.

She gave me a wide eyed look, but nonetheless started walking towards the table.

Selene Reynolds saw us when we were three tables away.

Her dazzling smile showed us just how happy she was that we'd come.

"Blake...Blake Rhodes?" Selene asked hopefully.

Blake nodded.

"Yes, that's me. Nice to meet you!" She said politely, offering her hand to Selene.

Selene smiled. "And this...is this your boyfriend you spoke of?"

Blake turned her smile on me, dazzling me with its brilliance. "Actually," she said. "As of two days ago, he's my fiancé."

Selene beamed.

"That's wonderful! Congratulations! Sit down, sit down," she urged.

We sat on the side of the booth opposite of her and her son, scooting and moving until we got comfortable.

Which meant Blake was under my shoulder, and her hand was resting on my thigh.

We were touching from shoulder to knee, as we liked to do.

We small talked for a while, but it wasn't long before I could tell Blake was getting anxious. Extremely so.

She'd never been the best at waiting.

And right now, with her foot tapping on top of mine, I knew she was near her limit.

"Selene," I said, interrupting her question about what we were getting to eat. "If you don't mind, could you tell Blake why you called? I don't know how much longer I can keep her curiosity contained."

Blake shot me a glare, but Selene only nodded in understanding.

Turning her gaze solely to Blake, she started speaking.

"I don't think you really realize what all you've done for me," Selene whispered, looking over at her son with her whole heart in her eyes. "But I had to tell you. Had to thank you."

"Thank me for what?" Blake asked in confusion.

I tightened my arm around her shoulders as Selene continued.

"A couple of months ago I called 911 because my son was having a seizure. And you were the one to get the medics there. You were the one who spoke to me, calmed me down enough to get my head on straight," she whispered.

Blake looked over at the little boy, and smiled. "I remember that. I had wondered how he was."

She nodded. "Well, he started out really not well. He was born with a disease where his kidneys don't do their job right. Over the next few years, we've been using all sorts of medications in a vain attempt at helping him, but then he had a setback, and all of a sudden he had renal failure. He was put on a donor list, but we never thought he'd get that bad…but it did."

The woman smiled at her son as he interrupted her, holding his page up for Selene to see.

"It's beautiful, honey. So beautiful, Holden. Will you draw me another one, please?" Selene said to her son.

Holden nodded, and dutifully got to work on his newest creation.

Selene waited a moment, watching her son with such love in her eyes that it made my heart long for the same.

Finally, she turned from her son, looking back at the two of us before settling her gaze back on Blake.

"Then, a little over a month ago, I got a call in the middle of the night." A lone tear slipped down Selene's cheek. "They said," her voice cracked. "They said they had a match for Holden, and that I needed to get him to the hospital within an hour."

She took a deep breath before continuing.

Blake's hand on mine tightened.

My guess was that she saw where this was going, and was bracing herself to hear what she knew was coming.

"I got him there in twenty. Rushed him up to the floor, practically shoved him at the nurse, and urged her to hurry," she sniffled. "It wasn't until much, much later…about four hours into Holden's surgery, that I heard how we'd come to get the kidney."

Her eyes closed, and her words practically cried out her pain as she said, "It was a police officer that'd been in a shooting. He'd been the one to give my baby boy another chance at life. "

Blake's breath caught as she started to cry, and I pulled her into my chest, kissing her temple as she wept.

They were happy tears, though. That I could tell.

"He's…he's alive because of my dad?" Blake croaked.

Selene nodded. "Yes. Yes he is. And healthy once again. Something I only dreamed about."

***

"Do you think my mom would want to know that?" Blake asked me quietly as we were driving home an hour later.

I glanced at her, and reached for her hand before saying, "I think she'd like it. Yes, I think you should tell her."

Blake's mother was a bone of contention for us.

Blake really would rather not have much of anything to do with her since she'd treated Lou so badly before he died, yet I felt that she'd suffered enough.

No one would know if they'd have been able to work it out, because fate stepped in and changed the course of every one of our lives.

"Okay," she agreed. "I'll call her in the morning."

"Good," I said, looking back over at her again to gauge her mood before I breeched the next topic. "You hear about David?"

She blinked and turned to me, the hue of the red light clouding her face in red shadows.

"No," she scrunched up her nose. "What about him?"

I turned back ahead as the light turned green, and accelerated through the intersection.

"He's leaving, effective two weeks from Monday. Got a job up north somewhere," I informed her.

She stayed silent for a few long seconds; so long, in fact, that I didn't think she was going to say anything at all. But she surprised me.

"I'm not ever going to like him again…but that doesn't mean I want him to have a horrible life." I caught her shake her head out of the corner of my eye. "But I'm glad he's going. He's got a lot of ghosts in this town."

I agreed.

"So … tomorrow I want to start looking for houses," I said, tossing her a look.

She grimaced. "We have a house. Mine."

I sighed. "Your house works for now, but I want room to grow. I want to have babies, and build tree forts. And your yard is the size of a postage stamp. Wouldn't you like Molder to have a bigger yard to play in?"

I knew that'd work. She loved the hell out of Molder. Even though he ate my boots…and the walls.

"Fine," she said stubbornly. "But I want a kiln."

I snorted. "As if I wouldn't agree to that. I find that when you're covered in mud, you're quite attractive and enticing."

She stuck out her tongue. "I already said yes."

"That's what I thought."

She growled at my comment.

Luckily we'd just pulled up to her place, where we now stayed.

Otherwise I would've had to endure the silent treatment. Again.

Not that she was very good at it.

Once we entered the house, she walked straight the bedroom where she let Molder out, and I immediately let him outside to pee.

Then I fed him, locked the doors, and made my way back to our bedroom.

I stripped off my shirt and started to sit down to take off my prosthesis when my eyes caught Blake in the mirror.

Half turning to see if what I was seeing was real, I gasped in horror.

"Please, for the love of all that's holy, tell me you're not using my razor," I said to her stiffly.

She looked up from where she was shaving her pussy and smiled. "It is. Yours works way better than mine."

I blinked in surprise, astounded that she'd answered me truthfully.

"You know it's my razor…and yet you willingly continue using it," I clarified.

She nodded. "Yep."

No remorse in the woman whatsoever.

"You do realize," I said, standing up on my one leg to get into the shower. "That that razor touches my *face*, correct?"

"Mmmm hmm," she agreed, going back to shaving.

"Have you ever used it before?" I asked slowly.

She nodded. "Every time I shave."

My mouth fell open in shock. Absolute shock that this woman...this crazy, exasperating woman, used my razor. The thing that shaved my face every single morning when I trimmed up for work.

"And you realize that that thing touches my face...right?" I said for a second time.

She nodded again, not bothering to answer that time.

I leaned back and flushed the toilet, eliciting an ear piercing scream out of her.

"What was that for?" She sputtered, as the ice cold water of the shower poured down onto her.

Her nipples hardened, and yet again, as always, my eyes zeroed in on those perky little buds.

"Stay away from me, you horny toad," she hissed as she saw where my gaze had fastened on to.

"And if I don't?" I taunted, staying seated with my prosthesis on the counter beside me.

She got out, leaving the shower running, and wrapped the towel around her chest, covering all that I loved to taste in one fluid motion.

"Oh," she teased, walking out. "I'm sure I'll find some way to get away from you."

Warily, I looked around, trying to find what she'd do to me this time, yet couldn't find anything wrong.

Shrugging it off, I stood, then realized that my crutch, as well as my cane, were no longer standing where I'd left them the previous night.

"Hey babe," I called behind her. "Have you seen my crutch?"

She laughed.

The bitch *laughed.*

"Oh, you mean these?" She asked, poking her head around the corner.

Then she lifted up her hands, showing me the crutch and cane that were in her hand, as well as my prosthesis.

I glared at her. "Give them to me, you wench."

She giggled. "And what do I get if I obey, oh lord and master?"

I started to hop to her, causing her to back away and start giggling once again.

I made it to the door to see her collapsed onto the bed wiping her tears.

"What are you laughing at, you little stealer?" I asked, hopping some more.

The moment I touched the bed, she started to rise, but I caught her ankle and pulled her back.

"Eeeek!" She squeaked. "Let me go."

Pinning her down, I said, "No. Now tell me what has you laughing."

She had to get out a few more giggles before she finally replied with, "Your dick."

I ground my erection into her hip, letting her feel the rock hardness of it.

Something that was a constant bone of contention between me and my dick.

All the woman had to do sometimes was walk in a room, and it was rearing to go for her.

"My dick makes you laugh?" I confirmed.

She nodded. "Yes, you jumped in here and all I could focus on was the way your dick swung with each upward movement."

I pinched her ass, and rolled her over onto her belly.

Then I pressed the tip of my cock against her entrance, and started to slide inside.

"So…who's laughing now?"

She sobered. "Not me. Absolutely, one hundred percent, not me," she said, pressing her ass back so I slipped further inside.

"I didn't think so."

EPILOGUE

Have fun. Be safe. Come home.
-Key chain

Blake

6 months later

"Let's go, I don't have all day," Grandpa grumbled, doing his best not to smile.

I fluffed out my skirt one more time, turned in a circle, and grimaced.

I looked like a beached whale.

At five months pregnant, there wasn't much a girl could do to hide the fact.

I wasn't blessed with one of those small bellies, either.

I was blessed with a large one. One that didn't hide a single damn thing.

"You're pregnant. Yes. You don't have to keep staring at it." Grandpa put in his unwanted two cents.

I stuck my tongue out at him, and finally stepped up to the door that led to the chapel.

"Ready, Freddy," I teased.

He narrowed his eyes at me, stopping me before I would've opened the door.

"You know your daddy was always real proud of you, right?" He asked, touching the tips of his fingertips to my face.

I smiled, cupping his hand with my own.

"Yeah, grandpa. I do," I whispered, a lone tear threatening to spill over.

He leaned forward and kissed my nose before turning back toward the door and thrusting it open.

The door banged against the side of the wall, effectively announcing our entrance just as well as the music that was now playing throughout the church.

Instead of waiting for the music to get to the right point, he started to yank me down the aisle as fast as his arthritic knees would allow.

"You know, right, that you'll have to spend the rest of your life with him?" Grandpa asked once we were half way down the aisle.

I giggled. "Yes, I do know that."

I passed Pauline and gave her a little wave before I, once again, got yanked for not keeping up.

"Come on, slow poke. Your man's a-waitin'," he urged.

I looked up into Foster's amused eyes, so freakin' happy that I barely contained the urge to run down the aisle towards him.

"Go on, you know you want to," my grandpa said, giving me a slight shove.

I stopped and pulled him to a stop next to me. Then gave him a loud smacking kiss on the cheek. "Thank you, grandpa."

He blushed. "Get on with it. If you don't hurry you'll be givin' birth in front of the entire God forsaken town."

I laughed, then started to run towards the man that made my dreams come true.

His overprotective self, of course, started to freak out that I was running when I should clearly be taking caution in anything I did.

And running definitely wasn't taking caution.

But I enjoyed seeing the panic in his eyes as I launched myself at him.

I had no doubt that he'd catch me.

Something he did effortlessly.

Even going as far as to cushion the impact by hunching his shoulders to allow more room for my belly.

He spun me around once before turning with me in his arms to face the priest.

A priest, who enjoyed the display of affection, just as much as the rest of the audience.

"So…I can see that we're all excited to be here," he laughed.

I nodded enthusiastically.

"Alright," he nodded his head. "I was told I had to read this before I began. So here it goes."

My daughter and the man that holds her heart,

I gave this note to your uncle on the off chance that something ever happened to me. He was to give it to the preacher on the day that you married. I only assume that he followed directions, because if you're hearing this note read aloud, it means that I am no longer of this world. And Darren always was a shithead who refused to follow orders.

The crowd laughed, my eyes, now watering, turned to Uncle Darren.

He smiled at me fondly, nodding his head, encouraging me to listen.

The day that you were born was the happiest day of my life. I never thought that I would ever have something so precious that was made by me. Of course, your mother had a hand in it, too. Yet, I knew, the moment you were born that you'd be my little girl. I'd teach you everything you needed to know to succeed in life. To mold you into the perfect person who'd make some man extremely happy one day.

And I did. And I know that man standing beside you is extremely happy. In fact, if he has any brain in his head at all, he's thanking the good God above that you were given to him.

Foster's arms tensed around me tightly. "He's right. I'm fucking ecstatic that I have you. And always will be."

From this day forward, you will forever belong to this man. There'll be days that you fight. Days that you can't stand the sight of the other. Yet, you'll forget about it, because you love each other. You will have a fight, and the next thing you know you're cooking dinner together and neither one of you will remember what you were fighting about twenty minutes before.

A word of advice to my son- in- law, she'll bring up things that happened a year and a half ago in a fight about what you want for dinner. It'll happen. Trust me. Blake is a shit when she's in a bad mood. Stick with her, though. She's worth it.

I laughed, wiping the tears from my eyes, thankful that I'd worn waterproof mascara.

To my Blake, I hope you realize just how much you meant to me. How much I regret not being there to walk you down the aisle. To give you away to the man that I know will take care of you for the rest of your life.

You're the beat to my heart, and I'm so proud of you.

I love you with all my heart, and I will always be watching over you.

Dad.

I hiccupped a sob as I turned my face into Foster's chest, grieving once again for the man that I missed with all my heart.

"The priest said 'shit,'" Foster said into my hair.

I laughed into his chest before I leaned back and stared up at the man I was about to marry.

I knew one thing for sure, and that was that I was one happy woman.

I was marrying the man of my dreams. I was pregnant with his baby. We had a house that was beautiful, and we both had jobs that we loved.

I couldn't ask for a single thing more than I already had.

***

Foster

6 months later

I walked into the room, tired as hell from a shift that went from eight hours to twelve.

I'd just started heading to a call when I the pager that I was forced to carry for any SWAT callouts went off.

Now, after a four hour long hostage negotiation call was over, I was finally getting home to my family.

I wasn't sure if they'd be up or not. Beckham's schedule was still pretty sporadic.

At two months old, she still got up every three to four hours like clockwork to eat…and that was if she even went to sleep afterwards.

I found my two girls watching TV.

Well…Beckham was in her swing, swinging away while she stared at the TV.

Blake was on her back on the couch, arm thrown up over her head while she slept.

She looked beautiful, even if she was still wearing yesterday's clothes, and was sporting a giant white stain on her chest from what'd I assumed to be spit up.

Beckham cooed as I walked over to her.

Turning the dial off to stop the swing, I picked her up and cradled her against my chest.

She smelled like baby lotion. The one in the purple bottle that was supposed to help her sleep. Yet, here the girl was, at 1:35 A.M. Still wide awake while her mother sacked out on the couch.

Not that I blamed Blake.

She did a great job taking care of Beckham.

Even worse, she'd started back at her job this week and she was exhausted. Which was why I also overlooked the drool that was leaking out the corner of her mouth.

Beckham and I went to her room where I changed her, read her a story, and then laid her down in her bed.

She only ever went to her bed when I was there to put her in it.

She was Daddy's little girl for sure.

Turning on her mobile that projected stars on the bedroom's ceiling while it turned, I flipped off her light and closed the door quietly.

Then I went back for my other girl, finding her in the exact same position.

Smiling, I started stripping off my things, starting with my gun, badge, and Kevlar vest.

My boots soon followed, followed by my pants and shirts.

Everything was piled high on the floor, but I left it there to get later.

My next step was to bend down and gather Blake into my arms.

She was only slightly heavier than she'd been before she had the baby, but to me, she was still perfect.

If anything, she was even sexier now with the added cushion on her ass and thighs.

Her breasts were bigger, too.

Exceptionally so.

That was thanks to the breastfeeding. Something that was a serious turn on for me, yet I'd never admit to it.

"Hey," Blake said sleepily, turning her face into my chest to kiss it. "I missed you."

I smiled as I walked into the bedroom, sighing when I saw the bed was full of unfolded clothes.

"I missed you, too. I put Beckham to bed," I told her before she had a chance to ask the question I could see brewing in her eyes.

Laying her on my side, I walked around to the opposite side and shoved all the clothes into a large pile, then scooped them up into my arms before depositing them on the dresser.

Those we'd get to later, too.

"How was work?" She asked softly as I sat on the bed and started removing my prosthesis.

I looked over at her to see her turned towards me, eyes heavy with sleep.

"Long. The man who was responsible for the call we ran held the woman hostage with a BB gun. We spent four hours there because there was no way in without putting the woman he was holding hostage in danger. Then to find out the gun that we'd been fearing all night was fake was a major blow. Needless to say, we were not happy. Nico missed his anniversary dinner," I said, laying everything on the floor before I fell in bed beside her.

Blake scooted over the moment I got into bed, curling into my body.

"I'm glad it was a stupid call, if it had to be any at all. It's the bad ones that make my heart scared," she whispered, voice heavy with the beginning of sleep.

"I'm sorry," I said honestly. "I don't mean to worry you."

She patted my belly lightly twice in answer before she fell asleep on me once more.

And once again, I was left feeling so full I could hardly stand it. Full of love for my wife. For my child. For everything.

There was not one single thing I'd change.

Not one.

***

Blake

3 years later

"Mom," an insistent voice said urgently. "I have to pee!"

I sighed, closing my eyes as I prayed that my daughter would forget that she 'had to pee' and just be still for another three minutes while we waited for Foster to get there.

Today was Foster's thirty fourth birthday, and I had an incredible party planned out.

Right this second, we were waiting for my uncle to bring Foster in from the car.

My daughter, however, had different ideas.

"I'm going to pee on daddy's rug, and you know how he doesn't like that," Beckham scolded me.

Chuckles from the other men and women in the room surrounded me in the darkness, and I had to stifle the urge to laugh myself at the ridiculousness of it all.

"Fine," I said, standing up with Beckham's hand in my own. "If you don't go to the potty, though, I will spank your little hiney."

Snorts sounded out among the room, I'm sure finding it humorous that I would even say that. The irony of it all was staggering.

Foster was the world's worst person when it came to punishing, and usually it was me who did all of it…which didn't happen all that often.

I just hated when Beckham cried, and she had the softest, most sensitive heart in the world. It was hard for anyone to scold her, let alone spank her.

"Mommy," she said softly. "I can't see."

I sighed and started searching for my phone, but Luke, who'd been sitting beside me, flipped his lighter open and turned it on.

Which was followed by the rest of the men in the room, including my grandpa.

"Thanks," I muttered.

"No problem, my dear," Grandpa said.

I smiled inwardly, pulling Beckham in my wake as I made my way to the potty where it was inevitable that we'd miss Foster's entrance.

"Alright, sweetheart. Hurry up so we don't miss daddy," I said hurriedly.

She gave me a look that clearly said 'don't rush me.'

The same look her father used quite often.

"Turn around," she said.

Sighing, knowing she'd never go if I didn't turn around, I did so.

Finally she went, and was pulling her pants up when she decided that maybe she wasn't through completely.

My head hit the door with a soft thunk, and I knew we wouldn't make it in time to surprise Foster.

"I'm pooping!" She sang, as she always did.

My head hit the door again with a soft thunk.

"Momma, you can't tell you're fat from the back."

Thunk.

"And you have something sticking to your butt."

Thunk.

"It's still there."

Thunk.

"Mom."

I reached my hand back and felt around, immediately finding the sticker that I told Beckham not to play with stuck to my ass cheek.

Ripping it off, I tossed it in the vicinity of the trash, and gave another head thunk on the door for good measure.

I really shouldn't be surprised. Beckham had a way of making even the simplest things often difficult, challenging and time consuming.

She was like her father, after all.

"I'm done," Beckham announced loudly.

Flushing, she washed her hands, dried them on the towel hanging next to the sink, and came to my side. Grasping my hand she said, "We can go back out there now."

"You do realize, right, that your daddy is probably already here?" I asked my little mini-me.

She scrunched up her nose, as if the idea that a party would start without her was a foreign concept that she couldn't quite grasp.

Sighing, I opened the door.

Extremely unsurprised to find Foster standing there.

His arm was leaning up against the doorway above his head, eyes directed at me.

I smiled. "Hello."

"Daddy! I pooped!" Beckham announced loudly, as only a three year old could do.

"I hear!" He laughed, sounding jovial.

Once she was out of the bathroom, he stooped, picking Beckham up into his arms.

I was flabbergasted, yet again, by their similarities.

It was inevitable that Beckham would have blonde hair, seeing as both Foster and I did.

But the curls…she got all of those from her daddy.

They were tight and perfect, just like his. They didn't frizz out the moment they stepped into the humid Texas air like yours truly.

Her eyes were all mine, though.

"Thank you," Foster said, bringing my attention away from Beckham's face to his.

I smiled, then shrugged. "That's life."

He grinned, holding his hand out for me.

I walked into his arm, burying my face into his muscular chest, inhaling the warm cotton blend and crisp scent of outside on his clothes.

"You're not fat from either side," he started, making me laugh. "And nobody saw the sticker on your ass. I promise."

I giggled, allowing my head to fall back so I could look into his eyes. "I love you, Foster, my honey boo boo."

He snorted and steered me around until we started back towards the living room where the party was now in full swing.

Our whole family was there.

And it was big.

All of Foster's extended family was there, as well as all of mine. Then there were the families of the men on Foster's SWAT team, as well as a few of his buddies from his time in the Navy.

Our house was filled with people that loved Foster.

"Daddy, mommy said Louis is six weeks old today," Beckham told Foster as we rejoined the party.

Foster's eyes lit, and he turned to me with a smile. "Did she now? I didn't realize that he was *six* weeks old today."

I blushed under Foster's hot gaze.

Today would be six weeks exactly, since I'd had our son, Louis.

Louis was Beckham's polar opposite.

Where I'd had a C-section with Beckham, I'd had a natural birth with Louis.

Where Beckham had colic and didn't want anything to do with me if Foster was around, Louis was momma's little boy.

"So momma's daddy's birthday present?" Foster whispered into my ear.

A smile split my face as I looked up at him with all the love and adoration I felt for him in my eyes. "If that's what you want, I'll give it to you."

Before he could reply, a barking from upstairs had him sighing and handing over Beckham.

"I'll get him," he said.

I nodded, taking Beckham to her grandparents, Micah and Sloan.

"Do you mind hanging on to her for a bit while I go get the food?" I asked.

Micah was the one to reach for his granddaughter. "Of course. Then Beckham can show paw how to work his new phone. Sound good, pumpkin?"

I rolled my eyes.

They spoiled my child.

The reason he'd had to get a new phone was because he'd given his old one to Beckham.

I'd tried to refuse, but they'd insisted and I, of course, couldn't take the phone away from Beckham when she so clearly wanted it.

Whatever.

She'd lose it within the month anyway.

On my way to the kitchen, I passed by Luke who was busy feeding Boris a cracker.

"Watch your fingers," I said laughingly.

He snorted. "I learned my lesson the first time, trust me."

He did, too.

Nearly all of them did.

It never seemed to fail that they'd stick their fingers in the cage to touch Boris, and he'd turn around and bite the shit out of their fingers. Then he'd laugh, *the little bastard.*

We'd had to make a new cage that extended up higher so no little fingers could be accidentally stuck through the cage's bars.

I liked Boris, but god help him if he hurt one of Foster's babies.

"Oh!" I said once I pushed through the kitchen doors. "Thanks guys!"

Mercy, Reese, Georgia, Memphis, and Viddy were all in the kitchen setting out the food when I arrived. Doing the very thing that I'd come in there to do.

"We figured you wouldn't mind the help. The lobsters are done, too. Your aunt fixed those before she headed out to the party," Memphis said, pointing to the cooked lobsters laid out along the entire length of the counter.

"Woo!" I said, pumping my hand. "I hate doing that! Yet, Foster asks for them every year on his birthday, and I can't ever figure out why."

"Because I like the way you squeal when you cook them," Foster said, kissing the back of my neck.

I turned and smiled at him. "You're horrible, you know that?"

He winked.

"Where's Louis?" I asked, noticing that he didn't have the child that Molder refused to leave alone.

In fact, Louis and Beckham would forever have a protector in Molder.

He loved the kids, and treated them as if they were his own pups.

He let us know when they were awake. Let us know when they were sick.

"Ladies," Foster said, grabbing me by the hand and pulling me into the office that was built off the kitchen. "If you'll excuse us for a couple minutes."

Startled, I looked behind me, seeing the knowing faces.

"Foster!" I hissed. "What are you doing?"

He shut the door and locked it behind him before unbuttoning his pants, all the while corralling me towards the couch that was in the middle of the room.

He grinned when my legs met the back of the couch, and then laughed when I turned my frantic gaze to his.

"What's wrong, honey?" He teased.

I shook my head. "We're not doing this here. Not with that many people in our house."

He grinned. "Oh yeah?"

When he kissed the base of my neck, and tickled his beard along the sensitive skin, I lost the ability to use complex words.

"Yeah," I gasped when he started to suck at the base of my ear.

"I don't see you saying no," he observed as he started to lift my shirt and bra over my head.

"Mmmm," I said, eyes zeroing in on how it felt to feel his hands running over my breasts.

He laughed quietly. "So you want me? Here? Now?"

"Mmmm," I said again when he pulled one nipple into his mouth and started to suck lightly.

I gasped, hips jerking in response.

"Fuck me," I ordered him.

His response was to turn me around, lift up my skirt, and bend me over the couch.

With his cock lined up at my entrance, he pushed inside with a low growl.

"That's what I thought."

ABOUT THE AUTHOR

Lani Lynn Vale is married to the love of her life that she met in high school. She fell in love with him because he was wearing baseball pants. Ten years later they have three perfectly crazy children and a cat named Demon who likes to wake her up at ungodly times in the night. They live in the greatest state in the world, Texas. She writes contemporary and romantic suspense, and has a love for all things romance. You can find Lani in front of her computer writing away in her fictional characters world...that is until her husband and kids demand sustenance in the form of food and drink.

Manufactured by Amazon.ca
Bolton, ON